THE BURIED SECRET

A RIVER WINERY NOVEL

JEN TALTY

This is a work of fiction. Names, characters, places, and incidents are the product of the author's imagination or are used fictitiously. Any resemblance to actual persons, living or dead, or actual events or locales is entirely coincidental.

THE BURIED SECRET

Copyright © 2021 by Jen Talty

Printed in the USA

of the romance grabs you emotionally and the suspense keeps you sitting on the edge of your chair. Great characters, great writing, and a believable plot that can be a warning to all of us." *Desiree Holt, USA Today Bestseller*

"*Dark Water* delivers an engaging portrait of wounded hearts as the memorable characters take you on a healing journey of love. A mysterious death brings danger and intrigue into the drama, while sultry passions brew into a believable plot that melts the reader's heart. Jen Talty pens an entertaining romance that grips the heart as the colorful and dangerous story unfolds into a chilling ending." *Night Owl Reviews*

"This is not the typical love story, nor is it the typical mystery. The characters are well rounded and interesting." *You Gotta Read Reviews*

"*Murder in Paradise Bay* is a fast-paced romantic thriller with plenty of twists and turns to keep you guessing until the end. You won't want to miss this one..." *USA Today bestselling author Janice Maynard*

HAVE WE GOT A STORY FOR YOU!

Dear Readers:

Welcome to Candlewood Falls!

Each Candlewood Falls story stands alone. However, the end of one story doesn't mean the end of your favorite characters. They can show up in any Candlewood Falls book at any time.

Candlewood Falls is a unique world of connected stories by different authors whose characters, business, and events appear in each others' stories.

Think of Candlewood Falls as a literary soap opera.

Be sure to check out the the other authors and discover which other books include your favorite characters.

Happy reading!

Stacey Wilk & K.M Fawcett & Jen Talty

BOOK DESCRIPTION

A broken heart that needs mending...
A wounded soul that needs answers...
And a buried secret that could destroy everything...

After years of fighting with her mother, Riesling
decides its time to mend fences, even if it means she
has to admit her mother was right. Moving back to
Candlewood Falls is a big step. Dating her boss is an
even bigger one and Riesling's meddling mother is up
to her old tricks, making things difficult, as usual.
When another buried secret surfaces on The River
Winery it will not only test Riesling and her new
relationship, but it might just destroy everything that
the River family holds dear.

Doctor Treyton "Trey" Jefferson wants answers as to
where he came from and no one seems to be able to tell

him that. Not his parents and not the doctor who made the arrangements for the closed adoption because he's dead. Trey's only clue is a piece of paper from the doctor with an address that came from The River Winery in Candlewood Falls. Trey will do whatever it takes to find his birth parents, including using his new physician's assistant, who happens to have a stake in the winery, to obtain information about the doctor who facilitated over thirty adoptions in the area. He has no idea he's about to unearth a scandal that holds the power to destroy the woman he's falling in love with and her family's business.

To Jennifer Probst. Thanks for being my wine girl!

Trey

"**W**hat the hell is this?" Treyton Jefferson shoved two pieces of paper in his father's face and glared. His entire life he'd looked up to his father. Admired him. Trey had done everything he could to make his dad proud. He believed they had the kind of father-son relationship that most kids only dreamed about.

And in a matter of a five minutes it all faded to black.

Lies and betrayal so deep that Trey no longer understood the man he'd called father.

Worse, he didn't understand himself.

"It looks like a letter. Addressed to me. And a note

from your mother to you." Andrew Jefferson took the papers and blew out a puff of air through his nose. "Where'd you find this?" His father ran a hand across his bearded face and leaned back in his big leather chair.

Trey eased into one of the wingback seats and rested his elbows on his knees. "In a box of things that Mom left for me."

His father set the letters on the top of his desk and arched a brow. "Mom died a year ago and you're just now going through that stuff?"

"I couldn't bring myself to do it until now."

His father nodded. "When she got sick, she wanted to confess. I didn't. She told me she'd written you a letter explaining everything and I looked high and low for this when she died. I never wanted you to find it."

"So it means exactly what I think it does." Tears burned Trey's eyes. He knew he'd been adopted. He didn't care about that. Genetics didn't make a bond between parent and child.

Love did that.

And his parents loved him more than most.

"You have to understand what Mom was going through back then," his father said.

Trey stood and turned his back to his father. He couldn't look at him. "Did she know when you handed me to her?"

"No," his father admitted. "She didn't find out until you were sixteen."

"Jesus, Dad. You bought me from some crazy country doctor who probably stole me right off someone's front porch." The crazy vision of a baby snatcher that danced through his head like a horror movie taunted him like a bad dream. Being a doctor, he'd seen a lot of strange things, but he never expected to be at the center of one of those odd stories that were told at the water cooler. "That's criminal."

His father slammed his fist on the desk. Three books flopped to the floor. "Turn around and face me," his father commanded.

Trey did as requested.

"It wasn't like that. No one stole you from anyone. Just because it was an illegal adoption doesn't mean that the parties involved weren't completely aware and in agreement. Not to mention doing what was best for you."

"Do you know my birth parents?"

His father shook his head.

"Then there is no way to know that because you were only thinking about yourself."

His father flattened his hands on the desk and rose slowly as his face turned red. "You don't know what the fuck you're talking about, son. You have no idea what your mother had to endure."

"I'm a doctor, Dad. I have an idea of what it's like not to be able to—"

"It wasn't that we couldn't get pregnant. We did that ten times." His father held up both hands and

3

wiggled his fingers for effect. "Ten times," he repeated softly.

Trey opened his mouth to say something, but he had no words. This he'd never heard before and his heart broke into a million pieces.

"Your mother had eight miscarriages and two still-births. After she lost the last baby, she had complications and she had to have a hysterectomy."

The last part he knew, but not the circumstances, and that just made Trey's heart hurt even more.

His father arched a brow. "Yes, son. We lied to you about why she had to have that surgery and why she couldn't have children. She was utterly heartbroken. All she ever wanted was a family. A little boy or girl to raise. She was a mother without a child, and I was desperate to give her one. So when I met Doctor Allison and he had told me he could make it happen and quickly, I took it."

"His office was on a fucking winery. That's really sketchy, Dad."

"He rented desk space there. That's not where he saw patients. And it's not like he adopted out a lot of children. He did this only for special cases."

Trey couldn't believe he was going to even ask this next question. "What does that mean, exactly?" He held his father's gaze. He needed to know if he would be truthful, or if he was going to lie. "What made you and Mom, and me for that matter, so unique that it had to be done illegally?"

"Doctor Allison helped either the really rich and married who needed to help their mistress and didn't want anyone to know. Or a young teenage girl who got into trouble and the family wanted privacy in dealing with the situation and also wanted to ensure that no way could anyone find out in the future."

Trey rubbed his temples. "First. That doesn't make any of this okay. Second. How do you even know this is true? That doctor could be lying through his teeth about how he came by the babies he placed."

"He helped a friend of mine who got his mistress pregnant. They were able to do the adoption quickly, quietly, and without anyone finding out."

"Wow. That's supposed to make me feel better."

"Yes. Actually, it is." His father eased back into his chair. "Perhaps what I did was illegal in the eyes of the law. But the woman who gave you up did so because she couldn't or wouldn't take care of you and wanted someone who could. Doctor Allison had a good vetting process, and I used my resources to make sure he wasn't the kind of person you're thinking he was because I didn't want to make my Callie a whole woman at the expense of someone else."

Trey's father was the owner of a large cable news company and Andrew Jefferson had a unique reputation. Most people with the kind of power he had tended to be ruthless and went right for the jugular when covering stories.

But not Trey's father.

There were many in the business that didn't think Andrew would make it or that his channel would ever succeed because he was seen as soft.

Weak.

But really, he just had a big heart and he wanted to tell the news and cover the stories from the perspective of the person sitting in their living room watching it. Not from those in need of ratings.

And thus far, it had been paying off.

So, Trey had to believe his father had looked into this Doctor Allison, but that still didn't change that this adoption was illegal and his father had just admitted there was at least one more.

Which meant Doctor Allison had probably been doing this kind of thing on a regular basis.

"When I expressed interest in finding my birth parents, you asked me not to for Mom because of how that would make her feel. I respected that. But Mom's not here anymore and you were only concerned about me uncovering this." He tapped the paper. "I want to know where I come from."

"I'm begging you not to pursue this. There was a reason your birth parents opted to go through a private adoption."

"You mean illegal."

"Call it what you want," his father said. "You start poking around this, you could possibly destroy lives."

"You're being dramatic." Trey took the paper, folded it in threes, and tucked it in his back pocket.

"Am I?" His father clasped his hands and rested them on his desk. "I own a national media company that has a news channel. Imagine what happens if you find out that one of your birth parents was a politician's mistress or you dig up someone else's case and turn someone's life upside down."

"You're only concerned about protecting your—"

"You're damn right I am. This story breaks, I've got to cover it and how ironic would it be that I'd become the story. But the reality is, I don't give a shit about it from yours and my perspective. I do care about protecting anyone who gave up a child and all the babies that were adopted out. You could set off a chain reaction that could have serious consequences," his father said. "You're my son. I love you. If I thought we could do this quietly and it wouldn't cause anyone else pain, I'd help you."

"I'll ask you again. Do you know who my birth parents are?" Trey asked.

"No. I don't. And that's the truth," his father said. "And I don't know anything about them either except what's on that piece of paper. However, I'll give you all the other paperwork I have if you promise me you'll keep this quiet. I don't want to hurt people."

"Neither do I. But I need to figure this out. I can't let it go." Trey slumped back into the chair. "I tried to find Doctor Allison. He passed away fifteen years ago. He hasn't had a working office in Candlewood Falls in thirty years and there isn't a single person related to his practice that I can find."

"Sounds like a dead end, son."

Perhaps his father was right. Trey's life had been picture-perfect. His mother had been kind and loving and honestly, he wouldn't have wanted anyone else to have raised him. His only regret was that he wished he'd had more time with her.

God. He missed his mom.

She'd been his rock. She'd been the one who had encouraged him to follow his dreams and go to medical school.

The only reason he wanted to know about his birth parents was simple biology and to maybe thank them for giving him this wonderful life.

"I miss her too, you know," his father said quietly. "I would have done anything for my Callie."

"I know that, Dad." Trey swiped at his cheeks. "Are there any other buried secrets I need to know about?"

"That's the only one your mom and I have. I promise."

Trey would have to let that secret stay buried. If only he'd opened the box a few months earlier.

1

RIESLING

"**Y**ou look so pretty." Riesling River adjusted the bow in her daughter's hair, wondering how the hell her mother had talked Ashling into wearing the damn thing along with the dress and the shoes. Usually, it was one or the other, not the entire package. The child was more of a tomboy than Riesling had ever been.

And a hundred percent more stubborn. Ashling once decided she was going to wear her pajamas to school. She literally refused to get dressed and got on the bus wearing a pair of flannel checkered pants and a top with a sleeping bear. It didn't necessarily look like an outfit that a child would sleep in, but still, Riesling worried that Ashling might get picked on at school if anyone knew.

Ashling's response to that had been, *I'm Weezer's granddaughter. I can take it.*

"Thanks, Mommy! Can I go find Zinfandel? She promised to play with me."

"Sure." Riesling kissed her baby girl on the forehead.

Ashling raced off like a bat out of hell, weaving between family and friends in the wine tasting room of The River Winery.

Riesling sighed. Being Weezer River's child hadn't been easy. Not for any of Weezer's seven children. They had all moved out of Candlewood Falls for a reason. Some farther away than others, but all of Riesling's siblings had begun to return home and make amends with their mom.

It was time for Riesling to do the same.

Only, in order for her to truly have her mother fully in her life, it meant possibly breaking her daughter's heart.

Riesling scanned the room. It warmed her heart to know Malbec had not only found Eliza Jane to share his life with, but that he'd finally come back to Candlewood Falls and had been able to put things right with their mother. The pressure that had been placed on Malbec had been completely unfair and he'd paid a high price because of it. It drove him all the way across the country. His ability to forgive their parents set the bar high for Riesling. What Weezer had done, keeping her father and grandfather's secret and putting a wedge between her and the rest of her family, could have destroyed them all.

Her gaze landed on Mister Jimmy Armstrong, who at one point used to be the mayor of Candlewood Falls. Damn, that man looked good for a seventy-five-year-old. Growing up, her mother always tried to fix Chablis up with Jimmy Junior.

It was never going to happen.

Chablis wasn't girly enough, according to Junior, and Chablis thought Junior was a little too shallow. What was funny was that they secretly dated for a year, but decided they were better off friends and have remained close even though Junior now lived in Alabama with his Southern bride and family.

Unfortunately, Dina, Armstrong's daughter, passed away when she'd been only twenty-three. He spun his wife, Nadine, around the dance floor.

Rumor had it that Armstrong had a few affairs, but nothing had ever been proven, not even while he'd been in a heated campaign for mayor of Candlewood Falls and his wife had always stood by her man. Nadine had once been quoted in the local paper as saying she thought it funny that for every man who ran for office, the public went looking for a sex scandal instead of focusing on what really mattered and that's what the candidate would be able to do for the people of Candlewood Falls.

She won him the mayorship, hands down, and no one ever publicly accused him of having an affair again.

"Hey, kiddo." Her father dropped his arm around

her shoulders. "I hope I'm that light on my feet when I'm Armstrong's age."

She laughed. "I'm sure you will be able to cut a rug with the best of them."

Her dad had this uncanny ability to keep everyone together, even when they all wanted to strangle each other. Had it not been for him, she wondered what might have happened the day Weezer told her it was her or Theo.

And Riesling chose Theo.

What a fucking mistake that had been, and Riesling and her daughter had been paying for it ever since.

She waved to Harry and Molly, who sat at a table across the room. She was surprised they had come, but happy for her child's sake. "Thank you for inviting the Richardsons."

"Are you kidding? They're Ashling's other grandparents and they didn't do anything wrong."

"No. They didn't. But I did." Every time she thought about the things Theo held over her head, she wanted to run and hide in shame.

Her father gave her a weak smile. "You've got to stop letting him control your life. What's done is done."

"It's not that simple and you know it. I helped him and he reminds me of it every time he waltzes back into our lives."

"No one holds you accountable for his actions. Not

a single person." Her father kissed her forehead. "You made a mistake. Stop beating yourself up for it."

"It's kind of hard not to when every time I think he might actually stay away, he shows up and uses our precious little girl, and he has every right to see her and there isn't anything I can do about that. He owes me nothing in the way of child support, and visitation—thanks to a judge who bought his sob story—was never set to a schedule. He gets to see her when it's convenient. Which is never."

"We can take him to court again," her father said.

She shook her head. "All that will do is bring him back into our lives. I don't want that." She honestly hoped he'd forget all about her and their daughter, but she knew that to be wishful thinking.

"Are you all settled into your new place?" her dad asked, thankfully shifting the conversation. He was good about that.

"Pretty much." She leaned into her father's strong frame. He'd been her hero her entire life. Even when her mom had told her she'd turned into her biggest disappointment. "Ashling is so excited to be living so close to you and her grandma and everyone else."

"We're happy about it too."

Riesling's chest tightened. While she and her mother put on a good front for the sake of Ashling, their relationship was more than strained. They hadn't had been able to have a real conversation that didn't end up in a fight in years and Riesling was damn tired of it. "Mom certainly loves having Ashling around, but I'm not so sure she's thrilled to be seeing my face every day."

"That's not true." Her father turned and gripped her biceps. "Your mother loves you. The second she found out you took the physician's assistant job, she went about helping you decorate the cottage you're renting."

"That's about Ashling. Not me."

Her dad lowered his chin. "She doesn't like the way things are between the two of you. But you know how she gets, and I know this is going to get me in the doghouse with you as well, but I do agree with your mom. Theo doesn't deserve the kindness you show him and he constantly breaks that little girl's heart. It's hard for me to stand back and watch it. It's even harder for your mom, but we've both—"

"No, Dad. She hasn't taken a step back and let me handle Theo and neither have you." Riesling sucked in a deep breath. "I know you have a set of legal documents asking Theo to give up all his parental rights ready to shove under my nose."

Her dad planted his hands on his hips. "Ever since Ashling was born, Theo has done nothing but be absent in her life and bleed you dry for money. I've bit my tongue ninety percent of the time. But yes, I have all the necessary paperwork drafted because if my calculations are correct, it's been seven months since she's last seen her father and I'm sure he's about out of money, which means he'll be knocking at your door, asking for more, all under the pretense he misses his little girl." Her dad raked a hand across the top of his head. "If he shows his ugly face in this town, I won't be doing my best to keep your mother under control because she'll be standing in line behind me to give that young man a piece of my mind and maybe a fist sandwich."

Riesling swallowed. It was rare her father got that emotional, much less that vocal about anything. He had always been considered the voice of reason.

"This is my life. My family. You need to let me deal with it."

"If I cross paths with him, I won't keep my mouth shut. Just being honest." He leaned over and kissed her forehead. "Don't give Theo any more money and I bet he will stop coming around altogether. I know you believe that because he's her father it's better than nothing, but trust me when I say, there is nothing worse than having a parent that is in your life and doesn't love you. It's better that he's not present." He waved his hand toward the center of the wine tasting room. "Especially when she has all this. These people are her family. They are the ones who will love and protect her forever no matter what. Hell, Eliza Jane has only known her for a few short months, but they have a bond that can't be broken. You can't say the same thing about Theo."

Riesling knew her father was right. She'd always

known that and the only reason she'd gone to bed with Theo was because he was exactly what her mother hated. He was a beer drinking, tattooed, high school dropout who represented everything that Weezer didn't want for her precious Riesling. At twenty-five, Riesling had already disappointed her mother by not going into the family business. She'd broken up with the perfect man. The one that her mother had handpicked for her in high school. Riesling walked into a biker bar, saw Theo, and decided it was time to show her mother who was boss of her own life.

Nine months later, Ashling was born and Theo was nowhere to be found.

"I'm not going to be *that* mother who poisons their child—"

"Just promise me if he shows up, you won't give him any money," her father said.

"I believe I've learned my lesson with that one."

"Good. Now, when does the new doctor get here?" her father asked.

"A couple of days. Until then, I'm running the show, so when was the last time you've had a physical?"

His father tossed his head back and laughed. "The last time I let you listen to my heart, you wanted to perform open heart surgery."

"Daddy. I was ten."

"My dear child, you were on your way to the kitchen to get a butcher knife."

"Now you're exaggerating." Though that hadn't

been too far off the mark. She'd always been fascinated with the inner workings of the human body. She'd opted to become a PA over a medical doctor for a variety of reasons, but mostly because she felt it would give her the chance to be more focused on patient care.

"Maybe a little," her father mused. "There's your mother. I better go parade her around the dance floor before she changes her mind and sleeps at her house tonight."

"Your living arrangements are so weird."

"I'm working on changing that, but you know everything takes time with your mom." He squeezed her shoulder. "Don't let things fester much longer with her, especially now that you're living in Candlewood Falls."

Riesling hugged her middle and watched as her dad swept her mom off her feet. Her mother gazed into her dad's eyes with admiration. They truly loved each other. However, the secrets that her mom had been forced to keep nearly drove them apart. Had it not been for her father's patient soul and ability to keep a level head at all costs, this family could have lost everything.

Well, that's not entirely true. Riesling had to give her mother credit where it was due, and Weezer River was a strong woman with a big heart.

She just had an odd way of showing it to her own kids.

Riesling strolled across the room to where her brother Malbec and his future bride, Eliza Jane, were chatting with Brooklyn and Caleb, who were also engaged to be married.

Love was in the air and that meant her mother would be in rare form.

Wonderful. She snagged a bottle of wine and a fresh glass from the bar.

"You four look absolutely parched." Riesling set her glass on the high top table and poured herself a good old-fashioned River family pour before topping off everyone's glass. "Cheers to both happy couples."

"Thanks." Her brother leaned in and gave her a kiss on the cheek. "Your daughter asked if as the flower girl she could wear overalls and cute sandals. She promised to let Grandma put a ribbon in her hair."

"That's my girl." Riesling raised her glass.

"Did you even own a dress as a kid?" Caleb tossed his arm over Brooklyn's shoulders and laughed.

It was good to see him smile.

Hell, it was just good to see the man after many years of not showing his face in this town.

"I had one. I burned it," she said. Of all the girls in her family, she'd been the most like her mother. Not only did she look the most like Weezer, but her personality was the closest between the quick wit, dry sense of humor, and inability to keep her mouth shut.

Except for when it came to Theo. Riesling wanted Theo out of *her* life, but the very thought of him never seeing his daughter and what that would do to Ashling terrified Riesling. She wanted to believe there was good in Theo. That he loved his little girl, like Weezer loved all her children. And she did. Like a fierce bear.

"You were always such a wild kid," Brooklyn said. "But look at you now. All grown up. And a physician's assistant. I wonder what the new doctor is going to be like. I hear he's young."

"And good-looking," Eliza Jane said. "Weezer looked him up on google."

"Are you kidding me?" Riesling inwardly groaned. She should have known. "What did she say?"

"You don't want to know." Malbec gave her a good hip check. "But let's just say our other siblings are grateful that she's got her sights set on fixing you up and not them right now."

"I can't date my boss and if Mom meddles, she's going to regret it."

Malbec and Eliza Jane laughed.

"Mom doesn't regret much," Malbec said. "She never does and speaking from experience, she got it right this last time."

"No one asked you." Riesling took a long sip of her wine and glanced around the room, grateful that Brad Wilde had decided to join the group.

"I have to be going. Thanks for having me," Brad said with a big warm smile.

She'd known him her entire life. While she'd had a crush on Caleb when she'd been a kid, Brad had been more like a brother.

Malbec stretched out his arm. "Thanks for coming,

man. The party wouldn't have been the same without you."

"Wouldn't have missed it. Text me. We'll grab a drink next week. Eliza Jane, are you sure you want to marry this guy?" He punched Malbec in the arm.

"I've never been surer."

"Brad, we were just talking about the new doctor," Brooklyn said.

"Everyone is talking about it. Like nothing new ever happens in this town. Well, I guess it doesn't." Caleb shrugged and shoved his hands in his pockets.

"They need something to talk about now that they can't talk about you." Malbec threw an arm around Caleb's shoulders and gave a tug. Caleb shoved Malbec away.

Riesling found the entire exchange endearing. She knew how hard all this was for Caleb. Moving back wasn't easy when you're an outcast.

Something she knew a little bit about.

"I heard that was why you were back, Riesling," Brad said.

"That's right. Old Doc Harden is finally retiring. I came back to help with the transition. And to celebrate with Malbec and Eliza Jane, of course. I'm encouraging everyone to make an appointment for their physical. That includes you, tough guy." Riesling poked him in the chest with a long finger.

"Not me. I'm as healthy as a horse. I never need the

doctor." Brad waved over his shoulder as he strolled out the door.

Riesling laughed. "I've got ten dollars that says he's in my office before the new doctor shows his face."

"Are you serious?" Malbec gave her a questioning glare. "Brad hasn't been hurt in years. I'll bet you he doesn't set foot in your office for six months, except for something routine."

Caleb rubbed his shoulder. "Considering my recent brush with bruises, I'll bet he needs a doctor in the next three months."

"I don't know him all that well, but my competitive nature is kicking in," Eliza Jane said. "I'll go with a month."

Brooklyn raised both hands, palm out. "I'm not betting against my brother."

"Smart woman," Weezer's voice screeched in Riesling's ears. "Although, he's bound to need a doctor at some point. I'll take that bet for one year from now."

"Besides my brother being as fit as a fiddle, he doesn't break all that easily," Brooklyn said. "I think you all should find something else to bet on."

"I've got a good one." Riesling's mother looped her arm around her waist.

That couldn't be good.

"Has anyone seen a picture of the new doctor? He's quite the looker."

Riesling pursed her lips. Her mom better not be going there. At least not with her. Not now. It was the last thing she needed between uprooting Ashling and moving back to Candlewood.

"I've seen him." Eliza Jane raised her hand. "He's not as sexy as Malbec, but he's not bad at all."

"Why, thank you, dear." Malbec kissed her on the cheek.

"And he's only a couple of years older than Riesling. I—"

"Mom. Please don't play matchmaker with me and my new boss."

"He's single. You're single," her mother said with a shrug of her shoulders. "I'm just saying it's a possibility."

Riesling took her mother by the arm and led her a few feet away from the crowd. "Please, Mom. I beg of you not to meddle in this part of my life. I took this job so Ashling could be closer to you and Dad and all her aunts and uncles. But let's not forget why I left Candlewood Falls in the first place."

Her mom furrowed her brow. "If memory serves me correctly, it's because you ran off with Theo."

"You made me choose," Riesling said behind a tight jaw.

"I didn't actually believe you'd choose him." Weezer glanced away. She fluffed her hair before turning back. "I don't want to fight with you. Not tonight. Not any night, but you don't make it easy."

"I could say the same about you."

Her mother palmed Riesling's cheek. "I love you. I

only want what's best and of all my children, you as a parent should understand that."

"I do. But you can't keep inserting yourself into my life in ways that end up pushing me away. Promise me you're going to keep a safe distance when it comes to my love life."

"You don't have one, so how on earth can I meddle in it?" Her mother had the audacity to smile.

"I'm serious. I can't have you playing matchmaker with my new boss."

"Relax, sweetheart. I'll make that promise as long as you bring him to dinner at least once." She raised her hand. "If the good doctor were a woman, I'd be asking for the same thing, and you know that to be true. It's the neighborly thing to do."

"Fine." Riesling knew when to throw in the white flag. Her mother could be relentless, and this was one of those moments where if Riesling didn't do as asked, her mother would get her way regardless and it would end up feeling like a date instead of a simple dinner. "But remember what I said. This is my professional life, Mom. I can't have you meddling in it."

"You've made yourself clear." Her mother kissed her cheek and practically danced off toward a group of friends on the other side of the room.

Riesling blew out a puff of air. She knew moving back to Candlewood Falls would have its challenges and if she wanted to continue mending her relationship with her mom, she would need to keep reinforcing her boundaries.

It wasn't going to be easy, but Riesling was determined for the sake of her daughter.

Carter

"She thinks I'm going to meddle in her love life."

Carter River stood at the end of the bed and stared at his wife—technically ex-wife—and let out a long breath. "Are you?" He tossed his shirt over the chair in the corner of the room. His wife lay on the bed, her knees tucked to her chest. She wore one of those big nightgowns that some would call a granny-nighty, but she was still the sexiest woman he'd ever laid eyes on. And even though he'd divorced her years ago, she'd been the only woman he'd ever loved.

The only woman he'd ever been with and the only woman he'd ever want to be with.

They might have had a strange relationship and many people didn't understand. But it worked for them and that's all that mattered.

"No. Yes. I don't know." She climbed under the sheets and fluffed the pillows. "I'm waiting for Theo to show his ugly face and fuck it all up. This is about the longest he's stayed away, and that scares me."

"I'm worried about that too." Carter climbed in next to her and wrapped his strong arms around her body, pulling her close. "I had the private investigator that I've worked with before look into what Theo's been up to lately and it's not good. Same old bullshit."

"That means he'll be contacting her soon." Weezer rested her head on Carter's shoulder. "Riesling is a strong woman and could easily tell that man to fuck off until Ashling sees him, and then because of the way that beautiful little girl reacts, Riesling can't send the man packing."

"We haven't been able to cut him off at the knees either." Numerous times Carter had reminded her of all the times they had sat back and watched as Theo came back into Ashling's life for a couple of days while he talked Riesling into money. "But if he doesn't show up this time, I've got a plan." And this time Carter was going to make sure he executed it before Ashling ever laid eyes on that dirtbag.

Weezer tilted her head. "Oh, really?"

"We're going to pay him off and we're going to make sure he turns over his parental rights."

"Carter. No. Riesling will never forgive us. Me. She'll think it was all me. I need her to forgive me. I need to find a way for us to mend our relationship. Things are going so well with Malbec. Merlot is coming around. Chablis is even talking about coming back. I can't have Riesling running off again."

"Honey, I'll make sure she knows it wasn't you. I won't let her hold a grudge against you for something I can't tolerate a second longer. She'll know it was all me. Trust me."

Weezer kissed Carter's chest. "I don't want her to hate you either."

"I'd rather that than have Theo break my grandbaby's heart again."

2

TREY

Trey stood in front of the main building of The River Winery. The letter from Doctor Robert Allison burned a hole in his back pocket. The note by itself proved nothing other than Robert knew someone who could help Trey's parents.

But it had been the note from his mother that had chilled him to the bones.

A few people left the building carrying a couple of bottles of wine. They smiled and said hello as they passed him on their way toward their cars.

He glanced around. The leaves on the trees had started to turn brown and fall to the ground. He hugged himself as a cool breeze hung thick in the air. Soon snow would be falling from the sky. His entire life he'd lived in a city. Trees weren't something he saw a lot of. Wide open spaces with rivers and waterfalls didn't exist in his world. He never thought he'd ever live anywhere where he needed a car, but he was committed to figuring out where he came from.

Pulling open the big wood door, he stepped into the gift shop. It smelled like a combination of cork, cheese, and the finest wines. He wished it were five o'clock.

He could use a drink.

"Good morning," a gentleman about his age who was stocking jams said. "How can we help you today?"

"I just moved to town. As in today and I was driving by and thought what a nice gift to bring my new colleague." He lifted one of the bottles placed on display. "Only, I'm wondering if she's related to the owners now. Her name is Riesling River."

The man laughed. "Yeah. She's my sister and you must be Treyton Jefferson, our new doctor. I'm Malbec." He stretched out his arm.

"Please. Call me Trey." He took it in a firm shake. "She told me her family owned a business in town. She didn't tell me it was the local winery." Of course, he hadn't given her the chance and he wouldn't mention that Doc Harden had filled him in on much of the local gossip. Besides, Trey needed to play it cool. He had a lot of information to uncover, and he had to be patient. This wasn't going to happen overnight, and he had no idea if anyone on the winery even knew what the good doctor had been up to.

"I'm happy to put together a basket of all her favorites," Malbec said. "Fair warning, she hates her namesake wine. She's the only one of us kids who does.

It's weird because it's a good blend. She enjoys our Pinot Noir with my mother's home-baked crackers."

"Your mother makes crackers?"

"My mom makes a lot of things. Mostly she makes us all crazy," Malbec said with a slight chuckle.

"I heard that," a woman said from somewhere up above.

Trey tilted his head and scanned the room. A woman with grayish shoulder-length hair strolled down a set of stairs. She wore jeans, combat boots, and a flannel shirt.

"Did I also hear correctly that this is our new doctor?" the woman asked.

"In the flesh," Trey said.

"It's pleasure to meet you. I'm Weezer River. Owner of this fine establishment and Riesling's mother." Her beaming smile took up the entire room. "Don't you go listening to my eldest son about me and crazy. Nor should you take stock in anything anyone in this town has to say about me either. Especially if it's nice. If you want to know something about me, come to the source."

"Yes, ma'am."

"Malbec, put together a welcome to the neighborhood basket for Trey." She looped her arm through Trey's and tugged him through the gift shop. "This one is on us."

"Oh. No. I can't let you do that, Mrs. River—"

"It's Weezer and just say thank you."

"I wouldn't argue with my mother. Not if you know what's good for you." Malbec went about finding different things from the shelves and placing them in a large basket.

"Make sure you still do a basket for Riesling. Get her one of those pies we get from the orchard. Sam Wilde brought some over this morning. She'll love that." Weezer patted Trey's biceps. "So, tell me. What made you decide on Candlewood Falls?"

"The idea of being a small-town doctor appealed to me," Trey said. It wasn't a truthful answer, but it wasn't a total lie either. When he'd finished with his residency, he hadn't wanted to work in a big city or have a large practice. But it would have been nice to have partners. It wasn't that he was opposed to a physician's assistant. Not at all. He found them to be knowledgeable and an asset.

But they weren't doctors.

However, Riesling would prove to be valuable in more ways than one.

"I wanted to experience something different and went looking for exactly this. It took me a few years to find it, so I was thrilled when I got the job."

"You're going to love working with my Riesling," Weezer said. "Do you like kids?"

That was kind of an odd question, considering he was a family doctor. Or what people referred to today as a general practitioner. He didn't specialize in kids, but he could certainly treat them. "I love them, why?"

30

"Are you single?" Weezer ignored his question and continued with her own.

"Mom," Malbec said with a stern tone as he set the basket on the counter and added a few more smaller items. "Aren't you supposed to be meeting my fiancée about wedding plans shortly?"

"I have fifteen minutes." Weezer narrowed her stare. "So, Trey. Are you single? Or is a lucky young lady following you to our lovely town?"

Trey laughed. "Much to my father's dismay, I'm still single."

Weezer held up her hand. "For the record. I'm not playing matchmaker. I'm just suggesting that you ask my daughter, who happens to be single, to show you around town," she said. "And on that note, I better go find Eliza Jane." Weezer scurried out of the building faster than bee chasing honey.

"Sorry about my mom. She's been looking forward to your arrival." Malbec shook his head. "And any other single man she can fix up my sisters with."

"How many do you have?" Trey winked. "In case Riesling doesn't work out."

"There's Chablis and Zinfandel. Both equally frightening in different ways."

"Should I be scared of Riesling?"

"You should run for the hills," Malbec said with a hearty laugh. "But less because of Riesling and more because you made my mother's day."

Trey didn't completely understand what Malbec

meant, but he didn't have any siblings, and after his divorce, he thought it best he stay away from women for a while. He pulled out his credit card.

"Nope. My mom said this one was on the house and if she found out I took your money, she'd try to fire me, which is funny because I actually run this place now. She just likes to pretend she does."

"I have a feeling I'm going to be thoroughly amused by your family."

"Let's talk in a week and see how you feel about that."

Trey took his baskets and headed out toward his Audi.

Stella.

He had no idea why he named her that other than he felt like he was supposed to give the vehicle a good strong name. Of course, people named their boats. Not their cars. Or maybe they did. What the hell did he know? This was the first car he'd owned since his wife took the one he'd bought when they'd married.

He pulled out the papers in his back pocket and unfolded them. He pushed the letter from Doctor Robert Allison to the back and scanned the one from his mother.

Find your birth mother. I won't be able to rest in peace unless I know she willingly gave you to me. I'm sorry. I know this is a shitty thing to do to you, but your father will never go down that road. He believes the doctor was telling the truth. And maybe he was. But I need to know and I bet you do too.

Trey sighed.

"Yeah, Mom. Now that you've opened that can of worms, I need to know. But this has also piqued my curiosity even more on who I am and where I came from."

Riesling

Riesling offered Brad a hand.

"I can manage myself. Thank you." Brad hopped off the exam table. "You can wipe that smile off your face now."

"No. I think I'll savor this one for a long time. Besides, I'm a few dollars richer thanks to you."

"I'm well aware of the co-pay."

"Oh. I'm not talking about the office visit fee." Riesling opened the door for Brad and guided him toward the lobby. The office was an old farmhouse that the previous doctor turned into his practice about thirty years ago. Doc Harden rented out the top half to either his assistant, a nurse, or someone who needed a cheap place to stay.

Now the new doctor was going to live there, which meant Riesling and Ashling could rent the two-bedroom cottage on the property or find a place in town.

She opted for the cottage, or should she say her

mother all but insisted. Not to mention it was close to town, near school, and it was dirt cheap. It was a quaint little place. Quiet and out of the way. A stone's throw away from the doctor's office, which was nice. But mostly, it was far enough away from her meddling mother that she wouldn't have to deal with Weezer all the time, but close enough that both her parents could babysit on a regular basis.

Which she needed because she couldn't afford day care.

"I'm not following," Brad said as he rubbed the brace on his fractured wrist.

"I bet my family that you'd be in need of my services before Doctor Jefferson arrived on-site."

"You jinxed me."

She shrugged. "Make sure you follow my orders; otherwise, I'll be sending you to a specialist for a consult on surgery."

"Now you're just trying to scare me."

"That's true." She nodded. "But I've always scared you, so don't be stupid, Brad."

"Yes, ma'am." Brad turned on his heel and stomped off through the lobby.

Strolling behind the desk, she checked the appointments. Since Doc Harden had retired before the new doctor had gotten a chance to get to Candlewood Falls, a lot of people had rescheduled, wanting to wait for Trey.

She let out a long breath. She'd grown up in this

town. People knew her and trusted her family. Even those who didn't like her mother, still trusted the River name. Her father was the local lawyer for Pete's sake. And most people used him for their legal needs.

But Riesling's reputation became tarnished when she'd run off with a loser named Theo Markus Richardson. Most people around Candlewood Falls remembered Theo as the kid who nearly burned down the church over two decades ago, with the preacher in it.

Theo hadn't known anyone had been in the church, and it wasn't like he'd done it on purpose. At the time, he'd been remorseful. He'd been a teenager and a bit of a rebel.

But who wasn't?

The thing with Theo was he'd never gotten over his childhood resentments.

That nearly made Riesling laugh. Neither had she, which is why she'd moved back to Candlewood Falls. It was time to grow up and put the past behind her once and for all.

But Theo's idea of changing his life was always a get rich quick scheme that turned out to be a get in debt faster and owe bad people money scheme.

It was a never-ending cycle that always put Riesling's life savings in trouble and her little girl's heart on the chopping block.

At least Brad had trusted her enough to come in and get an X-ray. He could have really done some damage had he tried to keep working, and knowing Brad like she did, he could have done just that. Resigned that the day was going to be a slow one, she decided to head upstairs and make sure the residence was not only in good working shape, but clean. Doc Harden had said he'd have it professionally cleaned, but Harden was a cheap bastard and that probably meant he'd do it himself.

She was halfway up the stairs when she heard the door creak open. She turned. "Hello? Can I help you?"

"Are you Riesling?"

"I am." She paused at the bottom of the stairs and desperately tried not to stare at the man standing in the lobby holding a basket from her family winery while sporting a pair of jeans, a long-sleeved black shirt, and a sexy unshaven face. "Treyton Jefferson?"

"In the flesh."

"You're a couple of days early," she said. "I was just about to go upstairs and make sure everything was ready for you."

"That's awfully nice of you and totally not necessary." He set the basket on the desk. "This is for you."

She covered her mouth and laughed. "You do know that's my family's winery, right?"

"I do." He nodded. "Your mom and brother helped me put it together."

She peered over the side. "Oh God. That pie. It's sinful and I'm going to gain like ten pounds eating it."

"Why don't you let me cook you dinner, and then I'll be happy to help you polish it off."

"That's very sweet of you, but I take it my mom and brother didn't inform you that I also have a six-year-old little girl."

"I was not informed of that piece of information. Though your mom did ask if I liked kids." He shook his head. "That said, I make a mean mac and cheese and we need to talk about how I do business and that can't all be done during working hours and I wouldn't want you to have to get a babysitter. So, what do you say?"

"I can't tonight. But you're on for tomorrow." She held up her index finger. "On one condition."

"What's that?"

"I don't know what my mom may have said to you or implied. But I'm not interested in dating you or anyone else for that matter." A thick lump formed in her throat as the word dating rolled off her tongue. Oh, in the looks department, Trey was all that and more. His eyes were this deep blue color, like the Mediterranean Sea. They were so intense it was nearly impossible to look away. He had light-brown hair that wasn't short, but she couldn't describe it as long either.

And he hadn't shaved in what appeared to be a couple of weeks.

But she suspected he kept his beard and mustache that length at all times. It was a good look for him since he had a bit of a baby face, so it aged him just a tad.

"I wasn't expecting it to be social that way," he said. "I'm sorry if I implied otherwise."

"No. But I bet my mom did."

Trey laughed. "She might have a little. Does she do that a lot?"

"To every single man between the ages of thirty and forty who sets foot in this town." Feeling a little less on edge, she leaned against the counter. "I do appreciate the basket. That was kind of you and so very not necessary."

"If I had been smart enough to put two and two together, I would have stopped somewhere else."

"No. This is perfect. I do love everything the family business offers, except my own name."

"I heard that too."

She cringed. "Well, just don't believe everything my mom has to say about me. Or my siblings for that matter. Hell, this entire town has an opinion, and every single one of them enjoys expressing them."

"I've never lived in a small town, so this should be interesting." He stuffed his hands in his pockets and glanced around. "Where is our receptionist and all our patients?"

"Anna has the day off. It was easy to give it to her because everyone rescheduled until they could see you."

He tilted his head. "And why didn't they want to see you?"

"Some did." Her stomach filled with doubt. Theo had taken money from half the people in this town and promised to double it in one of his early get rich plans.

This was back when she was pregnant with Ashling and he was turning over a new leaf. He even had the blessing of Weezer and Carter and that meant something in this town.

But the company Theo had gotten involved in was nothing more than a small-time Ponzi scheme. Thankfully, because of her father, no one lost too much money, but still. It had tainted her name because she'd followed the father of her child out of this town as everyone had done him wrong.

And not the other way around.

"But there are a few who don't trust me." She felt she should be honest. "In part because of my ex and in part because when I was little, I used to try to undress all the little boys in town to play doctor. That didn't go over too well with all the parents."

Trey tossed his head back and let out a hearty laugh. It was deep and rich and it filled her belly with warmth like hot fudge smothering ice cream. "I hope you're joking about the latter."

"I am," she admitted. "But I did chase everyone around with a stethoscope, trying to listen to their heart or get them to lie down so I could push on their belly. I had two strikes against me as a kid. My mother being *The Weezer* and me being the weirdo who actually had people believe they might have some rare disease."

"You'll have to explain to me about The Weezer but I get the whole diagnostic thing." His expression turned serious. He ran a hand over his beard. "The worst part is when playacting becomes a reality."

She was about to ask what he meant by that when the front door flew wide open. "Riesling," old man Koontz said. "I need your help."

"What is it? What's wrong?" She raced to Koontz's side.

He had to be pushing ninety at this point. He was hunched over, clutching his right side and panting for breath like a dog. "It's Ella. We were in town enjoying the warm weather. She got stung by a bee and we don't have her EpiPen. She's in the truck."

"Did you call 9-1-1?"

He shook his head. "I don't have my cell. Forgot it. I swear I'm as bad as she is these days."

"Don't you worry." Riesling pushed past Trey and into the first exam room where she found what she needed. "Trey, call an ambulance. Tell them we have a sixty-year-old woman with early-onset Alzheimer's having—"

"I got it." Trey held up his phone.

She nodded as she stormed out the front door. Ella should be in a long-term care facility. Hell, so should her father at this point, but they were all each other had and who was she to lecture either of them. She pulled open the passenger side of the vehicle and stabbed Ella in the leg before climbing into the truck and cradling the woman in her lap.

Trey was one step behind with an IV drip. "Ambulance is eight minutes out." He began checking her vitals and finding a vein while she rested her cheek against Ella's forehead.

The older woman's breaths were shallow, but Riesling had seen her in a worse state before.

Koontz stumbled out of the old farmhouse and down the steps. He leaned against the hood of the pickup. "Is she going to be okay?"

"I believe so," Trey said.

"Who are you?" Koontz asked with a dark tone.

"I'm Doctor Jefferson."

"Oh. Well then, thank you."

"You're welcome." Trey opened up the IV and pressed the back of his hand against Ella's forehead. "Now, if you don't mind, I'd like to take a listen to your heart." He pointed to Koontz. "What's your name?"

"Edward Koontz and why the heck would you want to do that?"

Riesling glanced between Trey and Koontz and frowned. "Koontz. Let him do it. For me. Okay?"

"Anything for you, Riesling."

Trey pressed his fingers to Koontz's wrist as he lifted his stethoscope. He closed his eyes for a brief moment and then locked gazes with Riesling. "Edward. I think you better sit down."

"No one calls me that, boy."

"Okay," Trey said. "Koontz. I think you need to take a seat." Before Trey could help the old man anywhere, he turned completely white. Then blue. And passed out. "Shit," Trey mumbled as he fell to the ground with Koontz. "Does he have a history of heart disease?"

"No. The man hasn't had anything other than a cold since he was a kid. Hand to God. But his kids have all been cursed, like Ella here. Diagnosed with Alzheimer's seven years ago. His son died of cancer ten years ago. His wife died five years ago of Parkinson's."

"Well, I think he just had a heart attack." Calmly, Trey began CPR as the ambulance rolled to a stop behind the truck.

Riesling held on to Ella as she slowly responded to her medication.

What a fucking shit way to end the day.

3

TREY

Trey rubbed the back of his neck as he stood in line at the Green Bean coffeehouse. It had been a long night, but old man Koontz was going to live another day. He'd suffered a mild heart attack; however, the damage had been minimal and he didn't need surgery. All he needed was to reduce his stress.

As if that was going to be easy for a man pushing ninety who was the sole caregiver of his ailing daughter who had no idea who he was anymore.

And of course that was a living situation, which had to change. Riesling had been working with them, but Koontz was a stubborn old mule and didn't want to move his daughter into memory care. She might be past that, but now he needed some help; hopefully Trey could find them quality companion care for now.

"You must be the new doctor," a gentleman

standing behind him said. "I'm Carter. Riesling's father."

"Oh. It's a pleasure to meet you." Trey stretched out his hand. "I believe I'm going to really enjoy working with her." Even though Trey was already tired of small-time life, he wasn't tired of Riesling. Nope. The worst part was she'd already crept into his dreams. Not a good thing either. He needed to stay focused on his task so he could get back to his real life.

Carter laughed. "She's a good PA, but she's her mother's daughter, that's for sure."

"I meet Weezer. She's charming too."

Carter pounded his chest. "Have I suddenly entered the twilight zone and no one told me? Are you sure you're talking about my wife?" He laughed. "They must be buttering you up for something."

"I have been warned by a few people to make sure that I stay on Weezer's good side."

"That's always a good idea," Carter said. "But her bark is worse than her bite."

"Grandpa! Grandpa." A little girl came barreling into the coffeehouse, dodging and weaving everyone in line with great precision. "You're not going to believe what Grandma just heard that has her so pissed she needs to teach Mrs. Chambers a lesson."

Carter picked up the adorable child wearing overalls and pigtails with a special patch of dirt on her cheek. Or maybe it was chocolate from the half-eaten cookie in her hand. "What have I told you about repeating things that grown-ups say. Especially your grandmother."

"But Grandpa, this has Grandma so upset she sent me inside and stormed off muttering something about how poor Lyra deserved a better mother."

"Dear Lord," Carter said, shaking his head. "I'm going to regret asking this but what did Mrs. Chambers say?"

"That Lyra and her boys are living like they might as well be on that show *Hoarders*. Grandpa, what's a hoarder?"

"Nothing you ever want to know about and I'm sure Mrs. Chambers is just exaggerating as usual," Carter said. "Have you met the new doctor yet?"

"You mean the sexy Treyton?" She made a smacking noise with her lips. "Grandma says he's got a nice ass and that Mommy should be squeezing—"

"Sweetheart, this is Trey." Carter smiled.

Trey couldn't believe that a small child made his cheeks flush, but he bet if he looked in the mirror, they'd be bright red. "I bet you're Ashling," he said, doing his best to contain his utter embarrassment at the hands of a six-year-old.

The little girl giggled. "Mommy's not going to be happy with me for saying that in front of you."

"I won't tell if you don't," Trey said and no way in hell would he mention anything about this conversation to Riesling. Yesterday had been long and rough. They'd had to jump right into their working relationship with both feet, and while it had gone seamlessly, Riesling was the kind of person who needed to be in control at all times and he didn't need to be a psychiatrist to figure that out.

Ashling wiped her brow and flicked her wrist as if her fingers had been coated with sweat. "Good call." She leaned in and lifted her hand over her mouth. "But Grandma would spot me a five if she knew I spilled the beans."

Trey bit back his laughter.

"Honey. Do you think you can be quiet for a few minutes while Grandpa talks with Trey?"

"I guess if I have to." Ashling shrugged. "Can have one of those strawberry drinks and a chocolate doughnut?"

"Of course." Carter kissed Ashling's cheek. "Zinfandel wants one too. She texted Grandma and said she'd be here soon. Go sit at that table over there. I'll be just a few more minutes." He set her on the ground and she weaved through the crowd like Speedy Gonzales. "That child is ten times worse than her mother was at that age and I'm just glad I get to give her back at the end of the day. I love her but she's exhausting and we're only a half hour into it."

"She certainly does have a big personality." Trey stepped closer to the ordering counter. "What kind of coffee does Riesling like?"

"This time of year she'll like that pumpkin brew," Carter said.

"How about you?"

"That's nice of you, but you don't have to—"

"I insist," Trey said.

"Same thing."

Trey ordered three pumpkin spice coffees, two strawberry sweet drinks, and a dozen doughnuts, but he made sure two would be left out for Carter and his spunky granddaughter. A tinge of guilt plagued his heart. He didn't like using anyone in general, but he had no idea what they knew, or didn't know, regarding Doctor Allison and the illegal adoptions.

So far, Trey hadn't been able to uncover very much. Actually, he'd found out almost nothing other than Robert Allison was a well-liked, well-respected ob-gyn and people were willing to travel a great distance for his care. If he specialized in difficult births, that wouldn't be odd, but he didn't.

That should have been a red flag to anyone and everyone, but it wasn't.

And there wasn't a single blemish on the man's medical record.

"Thank you so much for the coffee and treat." Carter handed Ashling the doughnut.

She'd settled at the table and had her nose in her coloring book.

"This weekend my wife and I are having a few people over. I'd love it if you'd join us." Carter curled his fingers around one of Ashling's pigtails and twisted gently.

Trey swallowed. "I'd love that. Thank you so much." God, he hoped this party would be near the winery. He needed to go poking around. The doctor used some building on that property as his office and Trey needed to find out which one.

If it was even still standing.

"There you are." A tall red-haired woman waved as she practically hip checked a few people in the coffee shop. "Where's Mom?"

"On a mission," Carter said. "Zinfandel, this is Trey, our new doctor working with your sister, Riesling."

"I've heard about you." She lifted one of the colorful drinks from the table and drew the straw to her lips and sucked.

"I hope it was all good." Trey wasn't sure if he was absolutely terrified of this family or mildly amused.

Or both.

"You saved old man Koontz. You're a real hero." Zinfandel shifted her weight. "What's not to like?"

Unfortunately, no one lives forever, and it was going to be a sad day indeed when Koontz did pass. But for now, all was good in the world.

"My ex-wife has a few things she doesn't like about me," Trey admitted.

Carter arched a brow. "How long were you married?"

"Only two years. My parents warned me it was a mistake. I didn't listen. I was young and thought I had all the answers."

"How old were you?" Zinfandel asked. "If you don't mind me asking."

"I was twenty-four when I got married and she left me two years later." Trey wished he could be bitter, but he wasn't. Dani hadn't wanted to be married to him; she wanted his bank account, and she didn't realize she was going to have to wait until his father died for most of it.

"I'm sorry," Carter said.

"I'm not." Trey should have known his marriage was going to be miserable when Dani had complained about the engagement ring not being big enough. She'd wondered why he hadn't traded it even a year later for something a little fancier.

She was always bitching about the way he spent money or didn't spend it, and when she found out his father hadn't agreed to pay off all his debt and medical school bills, she'd gone ballistic.

It hadn't been pretty and that's when he realized she'd never been in the relationship because she had any real feelings for him, just the money his family had. But the truly worst part had been how it affected his mother and right before she'd been diagnosed with brain cancer.

Carter lowered his chin. "But let that be a lesson to you—"

"Dad. Stop." Zinfandel chewed on the straw. "I'm not dating anyone currently and have no desire to get married at twenty-two. Don't worry."

"Just checking." Carter laughed. "Thanks for letting me use you as a bad example."

"I'm glad my mistake can be useful." He held up his tray of coffee. "I better get these back to the office before they get cold and Riesling gets all bent out of shape because I'm late for my official first day."

Ashling lifted her gaze from her coloring book. "See you tonight for dinner."

"I'm looking forward to it." Trey turned and headed out toward Main Street. He'd yet to find out anything about Doctor Allison or his illegal adoption.

However, he had some good ins with the River family.

Guilt tugged at his heartstrings. Hopefully they knew nothing about what had happened on their property thirty-five years ago, and he prayed they'd forgive him for unearthing any scandal that might tarnish their reputation.

Riesling

Riesling rocked back and forth as she stared at the fiery sky and sipped her wine. While it was always nice to have a night off from mother duties, and that was part of why she moved back to Candlewood Falls, she knew damn well this had matchmaker written all over it and she was going to have to put a stop to it right quick.

"Here you go." Trey handed her a piece of warmed apple pie with a huge scoop of vanilla ice cream slowly melting over the top and seeping into the warm gooey filling.

Her stomach growled.

She set her wine to the side and dug in as if she hadn't eaten two portions of homemade macaroni and cheese.

"I have a weird question to ask you," Trey said.

"I'm all ears."

"Ashling is texting me. Should I respond?" Trey sat in the rocker across from her and rested his plate in his lap.

She held her fork midair and glared. "How the hell did she get your number?"

"I assumed you gave it to her."

"Now, why would I do that?" Riesling asked.

"In case of an emergency."

"I have a large family. I don't need to add you to the list. No offense." Shit. Riesling didn't need to be a detective to figure out where or how Ashling got Trey's contact information.

Her fucking meddling mother who didn't actually give a shit about Riesling except how it made the rest of the family look. Something she'd made clear the day she'd left with Theo, the *scum-sucking leech* as her mother liked to call him.

Riesling didn't disagree, except that was Ashling's father and that child adored him, when he decided to show his face, which wasn't often. The truth was that Riesling was a coward when it came to Theo. On the one hand, she wanted Theo out of her life.

And out of Ashling's.

But she wouldn't—couldn't—break her daughter's heart to do it. She could only hope that Theo would do it himself. She told herself the next time he came around asking for money, she'd tell him no and the mere fact that she'd moved back to Candlewood Falls made it less likely he'd come around because of his family.

And because of hers.

"None taken." Trey polished off his pie in like four bites. He leaned back and swirled his wine as he stared out over the small man-made pond in front of the old farmhouse. "Anyway, your daughter wants to know how our date is going and if I need any pointers."

"I'm going to seriously have words with my mother. Again." She took a big gulp of her favorite wine blend, resenting the hell out of her family's welcome basket. Dumbest fucking thing ever, especially since everyone had contributed one of their favorite things in the gift shop. "You can tell my darling daughter that her grand-mother is up to her tricks again and that we're just talking business."

Trey rolled his head, catching her gaze. He had kind,

welcoming blue eyes. "I probably should mind my own business since I don't have children."

"That might be a good idea."

He laughed. It was warm like butter melting over an ear of corn. Everything about Trey was sweet and sensitive, like a doctor with a great bedside manner should be. She'd spent the day watching him and he'd been truly fantastic with all their patients. He was a perfect fit to replace Doctor Harden.

She just wished he didn't make her heart beat a little faster and remind her that she was a woman who hadn't had sex in a very long time.

"Three years ago, my mom passed away," he said.

"I'm so sorry for your loss."

He nodded. "She was a lot like your mom in some ways."

"No one is like The Weezer. Trust me." Riesling tucked her hair behind her ears and stretched out her legs. "I used to think my mom meant well, and maybe she does with my siblings, but with me, I don't know. I've never been able to please her or do the right thing in her eyes, even when I do exactly what she wants me to."

"My parents hated my ex-wife, Dani. They knew she wasn't really in love with me and saw right through her, but I couldn't. I was blinded by—well—I have no idea anymore. However, once we split, my mom made it her life mission to find me the perfect woman. Obviously, I'm still single." He raised his glass. "Not only did she meddle in my love life, but she used to hire cleaning ladies for me when I can't stand having people clean my apartment. If she didn't like my outfit, she'd buy me new clothes. She once canceled my gym membership and had me join one where the ration of men to women was more in my favor."

Riesling stifled a laugh. "You're humoring me."

"Nope. I'm dead serious. However, once my mom was diagnosed with brain cancer and the meddling stopped, I kind of missed it." He shook his head. "Okay. Maybe not the intensity of it, but I know she wanted what was best for me, and your family, while all insanely overbearing, at least the ones I've met, they love you and it shows."

"You're kind to say that, and I'm really sorry about your mom. But you don't know mine well enough to make that kind of judgment call. Spend a little time talking with people in town. Most are terrified of Weezer. They will paint a picture of a woman who doesn't know how to mind her own business and sticks her nose where it doesn't belong. The worst part, though, is she's a really good person deep down; I've just disappointed her to the point there's no coming back."

"I don't believe that." Trey smiled. "Could your little girl ever do anything that would make you feel that way?"

"Doubtful." Riesling understood where Trey was going and Malbec had been talking her off this ledge for weeks. If anyone had felt the same way she had, it had been him. Hell, their mom had chased him across the country with her crazy. "But it's still not the same. My mom won't forgive me for choosing Ashling's father over her."

"Is that what you did?"

"It's what she made me do." She sucked in a deep breath and let it out slowly. She couldn't believe she was having this conversation with a complete stranger. With her boss. Of course, she'd watched him get some of the most difficult patients in town to open up to him. She was surprised he hadn't been a psychiatrist. "I'm don't mean to be rude, but do you mind if I change the subject?"

"Not at all. What would you like to talk about?"

"Why did you take this job?" she asked. "Your resume is impressive and you had a great partnership in a large practice in the city."

"I was tired of being a cog in a big machine. I felt like I wasn't seeing patients or practicing medicine anymore. I needed a change and when this came across my lap, I jumped at the chance." He reached behind him to the table and snagged the bottle of wine, topping off their glasses. "What about you? Why'd you return to Candlewood Falls and take the PA's job?"

"When my brother Malbec returned, I promised him if he could make an effort to mend things with Mom, so could I. But the bigger reason is I felt like my daughter was missing out on family and regardless of my rift with my mom, I don't want her to miss a moment with her aunts, uncles, or grandparents."

"That makes sense," Trey said. "How do you feel about hiring a part-time nurse or two to cover when you need time off to be with Ashling or would like a vacation?"

She stopped rocking. "This office has never had anything but a doctor. You wanted an assistant, so here I am."

"I know. And I also know the two of us can handle the work, but it can't hurt to have someone per diem, maybe approximately fifteen hours a week, that might be able to cover things like when Ashling is sick, or you need to go to a school play, or I want to go home and visit my dad and you need help. I don't want either of us to feel like we can't take time to be with our family when it makes sense."

Her first reaction was that he didn't think she could cut it. Maybe he didn't. Maybe her mother had once again said something that made her look incompetent. She always did. But this was his office and if she tried to fight him on it, she'd look like a bitch. "I can put an ad in the paper if you want; however, I'm not sure we really have enough work or patients." Shit. She shouldn't have said that.

He tilted his head, running a hand across his tightly trimmed beard. "I noticed that there had been a lot of requests for records to be transferred to another doctor in the next town over within the last year. Do you know why?"

"Everyone loved Doc Harden, but it took him making a near fatal mistake for him to retire. His patients lost trust in him and left." She blew out a puff of air. "And I'm not sure how many people actually trust me because of Ashling's father."

"Why not? What did he do?"

It was a fair question and the right thing to do was to tell him regardless of how it made her look. "Theo grew up in Candlewood Falls. He was a bit of a rebel without a cause and took off after high school. He came back supposedly a changed man, only he was involved in pyramid and Ponzi schemes. There are some people in this town who lost a nice chunk of their savings."

"That's not your fault."

"No. But some don't see it that way when after it all came out, I left with him." She lowered her gaze. "I was six months pregnant with Ashling and I didn't want to be a single mother. He promised me he'd make it right. A month after Ashling was born, I kicked him out and it's been a shitshow ever since."

"You really think the people of this town aren't going to seek medical attention here because of that?"

"I'm sure there are some."

"Well then, we're just going to have to change their minds," he said. "Until then, I think that would be a good idea to find ourselves a part-time nurse. You and Anna can do the initial interviews and narrow it down and we can pick the one we both think we can work with. We do that and we can expand and run walk-in clinic hours. If the citizens of Candlewood Falls see we're dedicated to their well-being, they won't have a choice but to see you as the kind and highly qualified physician's assistant that you are."

She burst out laughing. She shouldn't be. All he'd done was give her a nice compliment, but talk about laying it on thick.

"I'm glad you find me amusing."

"I'm sorry. I'll take care of an'ad." She had to admit, his idea of opening up walk-in hours was a good idea. "But if you really want to run a clinic, getting hungry doctors looking for moonlight hours would really be a better bet."

"I'm not opposed to doing that, but we need to really go over the budget. Buying this practice has me strapped."

Riesling had no desire to have that conversation tonight, especially since she was still staring at an empty bank account after the last time Theo had wiped her out. "From what I can tell, this place will pay for itself no problem. But expanding is going to take some fancy financing."

"We'll make it work, I'm sure of it."

She swallowed. She'd heard that promise from a man before. "Well, I best get going."

"What time is Ashling coming home?"

"She's not. My mom is keeping her for the night."

Riesling set her glass on the table and stood, stretching her hands toward the sky.

"So, you don't really have to rush off then."

"It's late and I plan on going over to my mom's for breakfast before our first appointment."

"Fair enough," he said. "I was hoping you might have some free time Saturday or Sunday to show me around town and give me some history. It would be fine for Ashling to tag along."

"Do you like apple picking?"

"I've never done it before."

"I promised Ashling to take her Sunday afternoon. You're welcome to join us and we can wander through town and grab an early dinner if you'd like." She told herself she was just being a good neighbor to the new man in town. No one would think it odd that she took her boss for a stroll down Main Street on their day off, especially since he'd just moved to Candlewood Falls and didn't know anyone.

"It's a date," he said.

Her heart jumped to the back of her throat. She swallowed. "I wouldn't call it that." She hadn't meant to sound so defensive and by the way he raised his hands and took a step back, she'd come off even stronger than her voice had portrayed. "I'm sorry. Things in my life are complicated and I don't want to lead you on or anything."

"You're not," he said.

She cocked her head.

He laughed. "Trust me. If my life didn't have its own set of complications, I'd be interested." He stretched out his arm.

She shook his hand. "Thank you for a lovely evening."

"You should know your daughter expects a text on whether or not I kissed you goodnight."

"Please don't encourage her. It will only add fuel to my mother's fire and trust me, that's a place you don't want to be."

4

TREY

T rey leaned against the railing on the porch of Carter's home and stared at Riesling as she played cornhole with a couple of her siblings. The evening had started out incredibly awkward when he'd found out he'd been invited to a family gathering, but he rolled with it because he had an agenda and he didn't want to be rude.

So far, he'd learned that his house had belonged to Carter's grandmother who passed away five years before Carter had divorced his wife and Carter's parents had wanted to sell the place. However, Carter wouldn't allow it and he rented it out until he needed it for himself.

What Trey didn't understand was why Weezer and Carter didn't live under the same roof. It was painfully obvious they were madly in love with each other and according to Ashling, who had less of a filter than

Weezer, they spent almost every night in the same bed. Ashling just didn't specify which one.

But she did have a lot to say about her great-grandparents who refused to talk to her grandpa because they were close-minded and mean, but not like her grandma who was just misunderstood.

Something told Trey the little girl was probably right.

Only, he'd been in Candlewood Falls a week and he hadn't learned one damn thing about Doctor Allison or any illegal adoptions, especially his.

"How are you liking Candlewood Falls?" Merlot, one of Riesling's brothers, asked. Merlot worked at the winery as second-in-command to Malbec and was the third oldest, just a few years older than Riesling.

Trey had learned that Merlot used to be a probation officer until a week ago. Interesting switch in jobs, but Trey found everything about this family intriguing.

"It's different than living in New York City where people walk by with their gaze at their feet or on their phones, making sure they avoid eye contact."

"There's no hiding out in this town, especially if you're on my mom's radar."

"I'm more worried about your niece. Ashling's quite the little firecracker."

Merlot chuckled. "She's exactly like Riesling was at that age. Used to drive Malbec and Chablis crazy when we were kids."

"How so?"

"Riesling's a lot more reserved than she used to be and that's because of her asshole ex-boyfriend."

"Ashling's father?"

"He's not much of a father. I don't think he's seen Ashling in months. We try not to mention him around either of them. It honestly breaks my heart to see Riesling this way. Part of it is her relationship with our mom, but hopefully now that we're moving back to Candlewood Falls that will change and she'll be more like—can't believe I'm going to say this—Ashling." Merlot tipped his beer and took a long sip. "You think Ashling speaks her mind. Riesling was ten times worse. She once told Malbec his date needed to see a good dermatologist."

"That's mean."

"It was true," Merlot said. "The best part was she offered to give the girl a facial."

"I'm glad her bedside manner has improved, but it would be nice to see some of that spunk her daughter has." Trey couldn't believe what was coming out of his mouth. Besides having no right to make any judgment about his employee, he didn't know her all that well.

However, what he did know, he liked. Maybe too much and he wanted to know more about her, which made him feel guilty about using her and her family to find information.

"You and everyone else in this family," Merlot said.

"Can I ask you something?"

"Sure."

63

"I came across some information about a Doctor Robert Allison who used to rent a building or an office space from your winery. Do you know anything about him?"

"I vaguely recall a story about someone who rented space from us, but that was way before my time, or at least ended before I can remember it. My mom didn't like having strangers on the property and I believe that deal ended about thirty something years ago."

"What are we talking about?" Pinot Noir, who went by Noir, one of the twins, asked as he handed his older brother a cold beer and offered Trey one as well.

Trey accepted.

"That doctor that rented the building we use as overflow," Merlot said.

"I wouldn't know anything about that. You'd have to ask Mom or Dad. Maybe Malbec or Chablis might know, but we haven't rented space out for at least thirty-two or thirty-three years." Noir sat in one of the rocking chairs and crossed his ankles.

Trey was thirty-five and from his research, Doctor Allison would have been close to sixty-five when Trey had been born. Finding information on him was going to be like finding a needle in a haystack.

"Why do you want to know?" Noir asked.

"I was curious," Trey said. "I found some old files with his name on it and the address was the winery. That struck me as odd." He did his best to keep things as close to the truth as he could and he had found an old record, Ella's file, with the winery stationery on it, so he could produce something if he had to in order to keep the focus off himself.

No one, especially Riesling, could know why he'd really taken this job.

"Have you brought it up with my sister?" Noir asked.

"I just found it today, so I haven't had the chance." He turned his gaze back to Riesling as she high-fived Malbec, successfully beating Chablis and Nebbiolo at what appeared to be a very competitive game of cornhole.

"She might have some knowledge, considering her fascination with all things medical in this town," Noir said.

"You could also go look in the library. There are some local history books about the winery and local business. Doctor Allison might be in there," Merlot offered.

All good ideas. "Thanks. When I have a few free moments I might do just that. But buying that practice with that house with everything in it, let me tell you, there's a lot of stuff and when I say stuff—I mean—junk."

Merlot laughed. "Riesling tried to clean that place for you."

"What she tried to do was enlist all of us to do it and we did the best we could, but no way in hell were we going to get rid of stuff. That was your decision to make."

"I appreciate the sentiment, but you could have tossed just about everything on the second floor. It's crap. I'm not even sure Goodwill is going to take half of it."

Riesling jogged up the steps with a sweet smile.

God, that smile was going to be the death of him if he wasn't careful. He enjoyed her company way too much. Working with her was seamless. His nurse at his former practice didn't understand the way he wanted to do things. All she comprehended was corporate policy and that he had fifteen minutes to see each patient. One minute more, and it put her in a tailspin.

Riesling understood all aspects from insurance responsibility to patient care and how to play the two. It was a fine line, but quality care always came first. The best part was he didn't have to explain most things to her or guide her; she simply knew what to do next.

It was like she was a freaking mind reader or something.

But if Trey was being honest, he missed the city. He missed the hustle and bustle. The nightlife. The hordes of people passing by on the streets. This constant having to say hello and smile while walking Main Street and the fact that everyone knew each other's business was a bit much to take. He preferred his privacy.

He missed his big practice. He missed not having to

be on call every day. Sure, there were things to like about Candlewood Falls.

Namely Riesling and her adorable daughter.

And perhaps the rest of the River clan. Even Weezer was highly entertaining at times.

But this was a place you came to visit. You didn't live here.

Well, he didn't.

"If we're talking about the furniture, they will take about half, but I'm telling you, if you put it on the street the day before garbage day, a lot of it will be gone. There are antique collectors that come through town and take shit all the time. If they think they can make it new again, they will. Otherwise, we can call waste management and they can, for a fee of course, come take what no one else will." She took her brother's beer and swigged.

"Hey. I was drinking that," Noir said, shaking his head.

"Why don't you go get two more?" She jerked out her hip and smiled. "You owe me anyway." She arched a brow.

"I'll go get another round if you say out loud what I owe you for." Noir cocked his head and smiled like a two-year-old.

Having been an only child, Trey was more than slightly amused and he was dying to find out what the hell was going on.

She let out an exasperated sigh. "Never mind. I'll go—"

"No. I want to hear this," Trey said. "I'll go get everyone a round if Noir tells me."

"You're acting like someone is paying," Riesling said. "And you better keep your trap closed." She waggled her finger.

"You set yourself up for this one." Noir hopped to his feet and put an arm around Trey.

"You do this, I'm never speaking to you again," Riesling said under her breath.

"Promises, promises." Noir laughed as he tugged Trey toward the main door to the house. "You see, my sister confided in me that she's going to the orchard with you tomorrow to go apple picking. I told our dearest mother she's going on a date with you."

"What did Weezer say?" Trey probably shouldn't have asked the question. Dating his assistant was a really bad idea. The worst. And not just because he had to work with her day in and day out.

But because he was using her to find out about his illegal adoption without informing her of what he was doing.

Okay. He could remedy that by being truthful.

But when he did find out who his birth parents were and he had the answers he so desperately sought, he had no intentions of staying in this tiny little town. Nope. He planned on going back to the city where he belonged.

"You're lucky, she approves," Noir said. "Because if she didn't, you wouldn't have been invited to his little family gathering."

"Yeah. I noticed I'm the only one who isn't family. Carter told me he was having people over. I thought that meant more than blood relatives."

Noir laughed. "Welcome to the Weezer version of Cupid. Though I'm surprised my father is playing in that sandbox." He led Trey into the kitchen where he ducked his head into the fridge and pulled out a six-pack. "You seem like a nice guy." He handed Trey a fresh beer.

"Thanks." Trey cracked it open and sipped. "But why do I think I'm about to lectured by a man who's I'm guessing about ten years younger than me."

"You're what, thirty-five?"

Trey nodded.

"Nine years then," Noir said. "And I'm not going to lecture you. I'm going to give you some good advice, a few pointers, and say some things that others in this family might be too chicken to say."

Trey tried to imagine what it would be like to have a sister. He supposed he'd be protective of her with any man that came near her, but Trey hadn't even officially asked her out and that hadn't been part of the plan.

Riesling shouldn't be collateral damage.

"Okay." He swallowed.

"If you like Riesling, she comes with baggage and

I'm not talking her daughter, though that's a package deal, as is this family."

"We're going apple picking. We're not getting married," Trey said tongue-in-cheek.

"Didn't say you were. However, you need to know about her ex-boyfriend."

"Theo. I've heard about him and he doesn't sound like a nice guy, much less a good father."

"He's a shithead, and I'm being kind." Noir set the six-pack on the table and pulled one out for himself. He took a long chug. "I was in college when all this went down, but I knew that asshole. He grew up outside of town and he happened to take one of my best friend's parents' savings and invested it in a Ponzi scheme. Well, half their savings, but it was a good chunk of money and they still haven't recovered." Noir ran a hand across the top of his head. "That old man you saved. One of the reasons he hasn't put his daughter in a home is because he can't afford to because of that prick, Theo."

"Riesling didn't tell me that." The air in Trey's lungs flew out like a flock of birds on a mission south. He and Riesling had a long conversation about what to do with Koontz and his daughter. They'd also discussed her ex and the money. She never lumped the two together. "I mean, she told me that Theo had taken people's money, but she didn't tell me Koontz was one of them."

Noir tilted his head. His lips parted. "I'm a little

surprised she told you that much. Riesling is about as stubborn as our mom and she doesn't like to be wrong. When she left town with Theo, she was six months pregnant, and she knew she was making the biggest mistake of her life, but she did it to spite our mother. Just like Malbec did when he took off for California, or Merlot when he dropped out of viticulture school and became a parole officer, and even Chablis when she never used her degree and moved two towns over to become a firefighter."

"But you, your twin, and Zinfandel, you all stayed and became wine sellers."

Noir laughed. "We're younger and didn't have some of the same pressure. By the time they all left, my mom was doing everything she could to bring everyone home, short of telling Malbec the horrible secret, which was that Eliza Jane's family was actually the rightful owners of the winery."

"Wait, what?"

"Long story and it's all worked out, especially now that Malbec and Eliza Jane are getting married New Year's Eve, but we're getting sidetracked here." Noir took another long draw from his beverage. "We want Theo out of Riesling's life. More importantly, out of Ashling's life."

"That's not really your place."

"Maybe not, but you don't see what happens every time that man comes back. He waltzes in with his hand stretched out for money. He gets Ashling believing he might actually stick around, but we all know that's not going to happen. If he gets money, he leaves. If he doesn't, he still leaves, and when he does, he doesn't communicate with her at all, leaving that poor little girl wondering why her father doesn't love her enough."

"That's a shitty thing to do, but why are you telling me this?"

"Because my father got word this morning from Harry, Theo's dad, that Theo booked a flight next week from Tulsa, where he's been living lately, to New Jersey. Now, he doesn't speak much to his parents, so he won't be staying with them in town, but it means he could be coming for a visit."

"Still not sure what this has to do with me?" The last thing Trey wanted to do was get in the middle of a domestic situation.

Besides, he'd been kept from his birth parents. Regardless of the fact that his father had told him that he'd been given up, that they hadn't wanted him. How was he supposed to know the truth?

"We're going to be doing our best to run interference in hopes that Ashling never sees him. My father plans on paying him off and having him sign over his parental rights. Whatever it takes. I'm asking you as a new friend of Riesling's to let us know if you see this man anywhere." He pulled out his cell and held up a picture.

"I can do that." Trey might do a little digging on his own first. Not that he didn't believe Noir and his family. But Trey had been lied to his entire life. Sure, he knew he'd been adopted, but it had been illegal. Just because his father was told that his birth parents had given him up willingly didn't make it true. Before Trey could be part of separating a child from their father in a forever kind of way, he needed to know all the facts.

Though, this Theo person sounded like a real asshole.

"I appreciate that." Noir tucked his cell into his back pocket. "So, that was the part that my family would be too chicken shit to say. Now, here's a piece of advice for you when it comes to dating my sister."

"We're not dating."

"Good answer." Noir laughed. "She likes to be in control, but at the same time, she's never been with someone who's swept her off her feet. The few men she dated before Theo were all rebels without a cause. She tended to choose guys that would piss off our folks. And since she had Ashling, she hasn't trusted herself so she doesn't go out much. There was this one guy who was nice, but he couldn't handle all of us."

"What you're saying is you scared him away." Trey should really nip this conversation right now. Unfortunately, he was enjoying it too much and he couldn't understand why.

"It's a thing, really. We believe if you can't handle us, then why would you want to be in a relationship?"

"Makes sense." And Trey had to admit it really did. That was the biggest problem with Dani, outside of the money issue. There was so much conflict with his parents, not to mention her family didn't like him much either. It added for too much stress on a marriage.

"My sister is trying to work things out with my mom, but they are so much alike it's painful."

"I can see that," Trey said.

"You seem like a stand-up guy who doesn't take shit from anyone. My advice is not to lay it on thick, but to keep doing things like showing up today once you knew it was a family gathering."

"I didn't know that until I got here."

"But you could have left right after dinner, which was two hours ago. Instead, you've stuck around."

Trey shrugged. Guilt filled his gut. It wasn't just about Riesling. Though, if he were being honest, she did have something to do with it, but it had more to do with finding out about Doctor Allison. "I don't know anyone else in town and I didn't feel like cleaning out the residence until I know when my new furniture I ordered online is being shipped."

"Fair enough." Noir grinned. "One more thing. I might be one of the younger brothers. But if you hurt my sister, or my niece, I'll come for you and it won't be pretty." Noir lifted the six-pack that now only had four beers and strolled out of the kitchen, leaving Trey standing there wondering if he'd been run over by a train.

5

RIESLING

Riesling hung back as she watched Trey and Ashling pick the final few apples to bring home. Trey had put up with a lot yesterday when it came to her family and he'd done so with a smile on his face. He became flustered once or twice, but he held his own with the best of them.

Including her mother.

"Hey, Riesling," Sam Wilde said as he strolled across the orchard. "I heard you've been giving Brad a hard time for getting injured."

She laughed. "I was only busting his ass for bragging about not needing a doctor and then showing up with a fracture, that's all. But since I'm here, where is he? I hope he's following my orders."

"He's up in the office trying not to go crazy," Sam said with a slight laugh. "He'd rather be out in the fields."

"I'm sure he would, but I'm glad he's not. His injury isn't going to set him back forever, but he'll heal faster if he takes it easy."

"Trust me, he's being a good patient." Sam had been a nerd his entire life, but what always cracked Riesling up was that her younger sister, Zinfandel, had the worst crush on him all through middle school and into high school. Why? Riesling had no idea. Sam wasn't bad to look at. Actually, he was handsome.

Now.

But as a kid, he put new meaning into the word bookworm.

Actually—strike that—he was a science nerd and that was worse, in Riesling's book. Of course, she'd always gone for the motorcycle, long-haired, tattooed bad boy, but only to piss off her parents.

Everyone thought it was only her mother she had issues with; however, her father hadn't been any better. He was sweeter and gentler than Weezer, but Carter River could let down the hammer just as hard when he wanted to.

And he'd done just that when it came to Theo.

"Ashling has really grown."

"She sure has and she's quite the handful."

"I can only imagine," Sam said, stuffing his hands in his pockets and bouncing up and down from the cold breeze. "Did you hear that Lyra Chambers is back in town?"

Lyra was Malbec's age, so a good seven, eight years

older, but who didn't know that snobby chick. She'd been about as stuck up as they came.

Even worse than Racheal, Malbec's ex, if that were possible.

"Is she and that fancy schmancy husband of hers visiting her folks?"

"That's just it. She moved into that dumpy place near Brad. Alone. Just her and her two boys."

Riesling jerked her head. "You've got to be kidding?"

"Nope. I couldn't believe it myself."

"Wow. That's just crazy."

"I know," Sam said. "Well, I better get going, but I wanted to make sure I got a chance to say hello and that bushel of apples is on the house."

"You don't have to do that."

"Brad took care of it, so it's done. Enjoy." Sam strolled off toward the main building.

"Mommy!" Ashling came running with her arms flapping like a wild beast. That child had more energy than the Energizer Bunny. "Trey said he'd teach me how to make his mom's famous apple crumble. Can we go to his place now and make it? Please!"

"That's not quite what I told her," Trey said with a bit of a sheepish smile. "My exact words were that I'd be happy to make it, share it, and give you the recipe. She came up with the idea and I told her only if it was okay with you; otherwise, I'd make sure she got her own little dish of it."

Ashling put her hand on her hip and pushed it dramatically to the side. "I did my school reading. I can get up early and take a shower before school and you made me do all my chores before we came here today. I don't see why we can't go to Doctor Trey's place and help him make the apple crumble. You're always saying you need something new to bring to Grandma's for Thanksgiving. Well, here's your chance to do something other than a traditional pie."

Trey turned his back, but he did a horrible job at stifling his laugh.

The day she'd left with Theo, her mother had told her she hoped her child had the same personality that Riesling had so maybe she'd understand what it was like to deal with someone bullheaded. Riesling already knew what that was like. All she had to do was look at her mother. But when it came in the size of a six-year-old with an attitude the size of the state of Texas and the resolve of something stronger than bleach, that was an entirely different story.

"I can name one reason we shouldn't go to Trey's." Riesling lowered herself to her daughter's level. "And that's your attitude, young lady."

Ashling pursed her lips. Her lower quivered as if she were about to cry. "I'm sorry, Mommy. Can we please go over to Doctor Trey's and learn how to make apple crumble?"

"That's a much better way to ask." She kissed her

daughter's cheek. "Are you sure it's okay with you, Trey?"

He turned. "Absolutely. I'd love to have you both."

She stood, taking her daughter by the hand. "My friend Brad, one of the owners of the orchard, gifted us that bushel of apples, so we are free to leave."

"That was nice of him," Trey said. "Is he a special friend?"

Riesling burst out laughing. "God, no. He's more like a dorky older brother and he comes with the same warning label."

Trey gave her a sideways glance. "What does that mean?"

"He can be protective, like all my brothers, and a royal pain in my ass. But all in a good way. Brad's a good man."

"I feel a little guilty taking these apples." Trey opened the door to his spiffy Audi SUV, helping Ashling into her booster seat. He was so good with her and it shouldn't bother Riesling, but it did.

Any man that wasn't Riesling's father that had this kind of connection to her tended to get under Riesling's skin. Not because she didn't want Ashling to have positive male role models, but because the one man who should be the most important person in her life, wasn't. Theo cared only about himself and Riesling should stop pretending it was different.

"Don't. Brad doesn't give me apples on a regular basis and we don't give him wine either." If she were being honest, Brad was doing it because of Ashling. He was a sucker for her smile.

Most people were.

"I'll take your word for it."

She slipped into the passenger seat and buckled herself in. She stared out the window as they pulled out of the orchard. She'd left this town more out of shame than because she wanted to chase after a life with Theo. After he'd taken a fair amount of money from a lot of her friends' families and then lost it, she should have left him, but he swore he hadn't known his partners were full of crap.

Deep down she knew Theo had been lying. That they were leaving Candlewood Falls not because the company wanted him to open an office in Ohio, but because Theo had stolen the money.

Shortly after Ashling had been born, her worst nightmare had come true.

"You seem quite contemplative," Trey said as he navigated the backroads toward the old farmhouse he now called home.

She always loved that house. It had character that many of the places in town that had been redone no longer had. When she'd heard that Trey had decided to live there, a small part of her had been disappointed. She'd thought she might like residing in the farmhouse. But it wasn't her decision to make and the small carriage house on the property serves her and her daughter well.

What would be nice would be to build an office building separate from the original house. It wasn't like there wasn't enough land. It could be done closer to the main road and that way if and when Trey ever had a family, he didn't have to either kick Riesling out of the carriage house or have to force his family to live above his offices. However, that would take an enormous amount of cash flow and she doubted Trey had that.

The real question was, why was she even contemplating the topic? Trey didn't have a family and he'd given her a two-year lease.

Her home life was secure for the moment.

Something she hadn't had in a while.

"I was thinking about Malbec's wedding. It's right around the corner." Total lie but now that she'd brought it up, her mind snapped to the happy occasion. Eliza Jane was the perfect partner in life for her brother. They complemented each other like apples and ice cream.

"I'm going to be the flower girl," Ashling called from the back seat with enormous pride. "I even promised to wear a dress and everything."

"I'm sure you'll look beautiful," Trey said.

"I don't really want to be pretty." Ashling's voice had that edge it got whenever anyone brought attention to the way she looked.

Riesling understood that her daughter didn't like it when people called attention to only her good looks, but what she didn't understand was why had she developed this at such a young age. For Riesling it was because she always hated walking into a room and having men turn their heads and deciding her worth based on her looks. Hell, even women did that and it made her crazy. Theo used to tell her all the time to use the assets that God gave her to get ahead in life. Silly her thought he meant her brains.

Not her tits.

"Why not?" Trey asked. "What's wrong with being pretty? Your mom is absolutely gorgeous."

"So is Grandma, but no one would ever say that about her. They always say she's smart and tough as nails and no one messes with The Weezer. I don't want anyone to take advantage of me."

Riesling sucked in a shallow breath. She glanced at Trey and then over her shoulder. "Do you think that if you're a pretty little girl that people will assume you're a pushover?"

Ashling nodded her head wildly up and down.

"Where on earth did you get that idea?"

"Watching and listening at the salon with Grandma," Ashling said. "All the pretty ladies with nice clothes and painted toes and nails all talk about how their husbands or boyfriends don't respect them and I look at Grandma and maybe some people don't like her, but Grandpa thinks she's the best thing ever. He says she's the smartest person he's ever met and even mean old Mrs. Chambers once said that my grandma has the kind of respect in this town she wished she had."

Riesling blinked. Her daughter had started talking at an early age. Walked at nine months. Her kindergarten teacher didn't know what to do with her half the time and now in the first grade, she was reading at a second-grade level and doing advanced math. She wasn't a genius, but she was smart.

And way too articulate for her own age.

But Riesling hadn't realized how intuitive she'd been as well.

"Grandma doesn't downplay her looks because she thinks it will gain her respect or that people will see her for being smart," Riesling said. Shit. How did she explain this to a small child without making it sound even more fucked up than it was? Because Riesling's mother had her own set of issues growing up that had made her into the woman she was today. Riesling understood them because in part, she'd done the same thing, though for very different reasons. "She gets her hair done weekly. Her makeup is always perfect and her nails are always polished."

"That's not what people see," Ashling practically shouted.

"I understand that, honey." Riesling twisted in the front seat so she could hold her daughter's gaze. "Growing up, Grandma wasn't allowed to be herself. She had to be stronger and tougher than the next person. There was a lot of pressure on her and she felt like her parents only saw this pretty little girl that looked like she could be in beauty pageants. She was told that being pretty made her soft and it made her look weak. So, your grandma, she became this big old personality that no one, except maybe your grandpa, even tried to understand. It was as if she was daring the world to see past her good looks, only it backfired a little bit because Grandma came on a little too strong."

"I like Grandma just the way she is," Ashling said as she sat up taller in her booster seat. "I want to be like her when I grow up."

Riesling's first thought was *oh no, you don't*. But she wouldn't be like her mother. She wouldn't stifle her daughter. Besides, Weezer wasn't the worst person in the world and that was something Riesling had to come to terms with. Because Riesling's life hadn't turned out this way because of her mother.

It had become shit because of the decisions Riesling made.

Regardless of the ultimatum her parents had given her.

"That's not a bad thing to aspire to," Riesling said. "But I want you to grow up to be Ashling River. I want you to be your own person. No one else. If that means you go through life with dirt on your face, then so be it. Or if you decide to be a beauty queen, then I'm right there with you."

Ashling scrunched up her face. "I don't know why or how Grandma does it, but I do *not* want to sit in a salon once a week and have someone fiddle with my hair."

Riesling smiled. "Then you won't. You'll find your own thing."

"That's right," Trey piped in. "We all have a thing."

"What's your thing?" Ashling asked.

Trey turned into the driveway to the old farm-house. "I love to cook and bake. A lot. So much so that I need to find people to do it for because I make too much for one person. Like this morning I made two huge breakfast casseroles, so I brought one into town and gave one to the Kyle family. I thought they could use a pick-me-up after the scare they had yesterday."

"That was real sweet of you," Riesling said.

"I have one for you and Ashling too." He pushed the gear shift into park, turned off the vehicle, and jumped out of the SUV, racing around the hood as if the Audi were on fire. He opened the passenger side door. "I've got a pot roast in the crockpot and there's enough to feed an army, so you might as well stay for dinner."

"Mommy? Can we? Please?"

"Since all I have is peanut butter and jelly, the answer is an absolute yes." She was going to get fat hanging around this man. She glanced at her watch while Trey ducked his head into the back of his vehicle and helped Ashling out of her booster seat. "But I insist on doing all the cleanup."

"I'm not going to argue." Trey took Ashling by the hand. "Let's get started on peeling these apples."

"I'm good at doing that." Ashling glanced up at Trey and smiled. "Better wash our hands first."

Riesling took the bushel of apples and followed Trey and her daughter up the porch and into the back staircase that led to the apartment above the doctor's offices. Outside of her father and her brothers, Ashling hadn't had many decent role models. It was nice to see her bond with Trey, though she would have to have a chat with him about keeping a safe distance. Not that she didn't want them to have a relationship. She did. Trey was Riesling's boss and one didn't buy a small practice like this if they didn't plan on sticking around. She wasn't concerned about Trey running off.

But Riesling needed to make sure he understood his place. They weren't dating.

They were co-workers.

And friends.

Hopefully good ones.

6

TREY

D inner and the baking of apple crumble had been a huge success. That is if success was defined by two ladies having huge smiles on their faces and no longer being hungry.

But Trey had more to do this evening if he was going to truly call the night a triumph in his book.

"You really don't have to walk us home," Riesling said as she strolled down the porch steps.

"It's getting dark and just because the cottage is only around the bend, I wouldn't feel right about letting you walk home alone."

"But I do it all the time." She laughed, tucking her hair behind her ears.

"Not in the dark you don't, and I won't ever let you either."

"We don't live in the city. People around here don't even lock their doors."

He glanced over his shoulder, scanning the wooded area. "You shouldn't say that out loud. Someone could be lurking."

"Oh, please. The only one that could possibly be hiding out in these bushes would be my mother. And if she were, it would be to make sure you kiss me good-night." Riesling paused and held up her hand. "That's not an invitation."

"Bummer, because I was planning on it." He curled his fingers through hers and refused to let go as he swung their arms back and forth. "Don't run too far ahead," he called to Ashling. "We need to be able to see you."

"I appreciate the way you are with my daughter. But she's mine to parent, not yours."

"I'm sorry. I didn't mean to overstep my bounds. I'm not used to country life." He enjoyed the warmth of Riesling's skin pressed firmly against his. It had been a long time since he spent this much time with a member of the opposite sex and didn't feel as though he was either being interviewed for the billionaires' ball or was being questioned about where a second and third home should be purchased.

As if any of that mattered when finding a suitable partner in life.

Of course, if Riesling found out what kind of money he really had, she might think differently of him.

Everyone did eventually. Even if they said they didn't.

Money changed everything.

"In the city, when I'm with my friends and their kids, they keep them on a leash. Literally."

"That sounds cruel."

"It is, but it isn't," he admitted. "One false step into the street, and they can get hit by a car. Or if they get too far ahead, they can get lost in the crowd." He smiled, watching Ashling skip across the lawn that was in need of a good mowing. He guessed as landlord that was on him. "The city, for the most part, is relatively safe to wander around during the day. But still, it can be difficult and dangerous to navigate especially for children."

Riesling waved her hand out in front of them as if she were displaying something. "As you can see, this isn't the city."

He laughed. "Point taken." He gave her other hand a firm squeeze. "Can I ask you something?"

"Sure."

"What do you know about a Doctor Robert Allison?"

"Very little, why?"

"He's listed as the ob-gyn on Ella's records and I thought it interesting that his office address was your family's winery." There. He'd asked Riesling the question. If she didn't have much information, maybe he could pique her curiosity enough to help him investigate the situation.

He was going to go straight to hell, if there was such a place.

"I never understood that." Riesling climbed the five steps on the front porch of the small cottage. She waved to Ashling who put her head down and slumped her shoulders.

Ashling moved slower than dirt, but she made her way toward the house where Riesling told her with a firm tone to get ready for bed. Ashling didn't argue, but she didn't look very happy about the situation either.

Trey gave the little girl a hug and kiss before she padded up the stairs.

Riesling let out a long breath. "Would you like a glass of wine?"

"I'd love one, thanks." Trey should leave, but if he could keep Riesling talking, then he'd have an entire bottle. "I have to be honest; it seems really weird that he'd keep an office on the winery, but that's not where he examined patients."

"I know. I'd want my office to be next to my exam rooms, though not sure I'd want to live where I work." She took down two stem glasses from a small bar next to the kitchen and poured some red wine. She handed one to him and clanked her glass against his before taking a sip. "Give me ten minutes to tuck Ashling in. It's a nice night. Why don't we sit outside."

"Sounds good, but do you mind if I use your little boys' room?"

"Be my guest. It's the door behind the kitchen. You can't miss it."

He waited until she was halfway up the stairs before he set his glass on the counter and went poking around, open and closing the drawers. He had no idea what he was looking for, if anything, and he felt like a real asshole. If anyone knew about what Doctor Allison had been up to, it would have been her mother, and he would have a conversation or two with her at some point, but he couldn't come on that strong.

Not yet.

He lifted his glass and made his way into the family room, which had been nicely decorated with an off-white sofa, a matching oversized chair and ottoman, along with tilted coffee and end tables. She had family photos of her, Ashling, and all her siblings, along with her parents, and what he assumed were grandparents all over the walls and bookshelves.

For someone who said she didn't have that great of a relationship with her mom, she sure had a ton of pictures of her and not of Weezer with the family. He picked up a framed image of Riesling and her mom, just the two of them. Riesling was wearing her lab coat and a stethoscope around her neck, with a beaming smile.

Weezer's smile was even brighter.

Trey set the picture down and headed outside where he made himself comfortable on the one of the Adirondack chairs. Slowly, he sipped his wine and enjoyed the sweet music the crickets made, something he almost never heard in the city.

"That child's head hit the pillow and she was out like a light." Riesling pushed open the door and eased herself into the chair across from him. She dropped her head back and sighed. "She's one energetic kid."

"You can say that again." He raised his glass. "But she's also one of the sweetest little girls I've ever met."

"Thank you for saying that."

"I mean it." And Trey wasn't lying. If he ever had a daughter, he'd hope she'd be something like Ashling with a mind completely of her own. He admired her fearlessness and her thirst for knowledge. Something he could relate to. "I'm sorry if I'm being weird by circling back to this, but Ella's record wasn't the only one I found with Doctor Robert Allison listed as the ob-gyn with the winery as the local office address."

"I don't find it all that strange." She leaned back and stretched out her legs.

He got the impression it was hard for her to relax. He resented her ex for putting her on edge. It was a difficult place to live on a regular basis.

"Malbec and Chablis used to and even Merlot used to tell me they would see our grandpa digging in the ground around the building we now use for overflow that used to be Doctor Allison's office. They thought it was odd and told our mom about it who asked her dad who in turn said that Grandpa lost his mind and thought someone had buried secrets on his land. Only, now we know there are secrets and while Grandpa, in the end, did have a memory problem, he kept some serious secrets from his family."

"Like the fact that the winery belonged to Eliza Jane."

"That was one she was expected to keep." Riesling nodded. "But there are more. We don't know what they are, and we're not sure we ever want to unearth them; however, we all know when they come out, depending on how bad they are, it could hurt us."

He set his wine on the floor by his feet and leaned forward. "I'm intrigued. I love a good mystery. Don't you want to know what your grandpa was looking for and what the doctor might have buried out there?"

"I never said the doctor did any such thing." Riesling arched a brow.

The corners of his mouth tugged into a smile. He shouldn't be happy about her calling out his mistake.

But he was because it meant he could draw her into helping him without her ever knowing he'd been a victim. He should also feel like a shitty person.

His heart dropped to the pit of his stomach and his half grin quickly turned to a frown. He cleared his throat. "I have a confession to make."

Her lips touched the edge of her wineglass. The red liquid flowed into her mouth.

He was mesmerized by the motion and couldn't tear his gaze away.

"I'm listening," she said.

"When I told my dad I bought this practice, he was shocked in part because he didn't think I'd ever leave the city. I've always loved living there. So does he. But more so because of what a small world it is."

"How so?"

"My dad has this friend who about forty years ago got his mistress pregnant. This friend used to be a well-known television personality, so he couldn't afford for anyone to know, but his girlfriend waited too long to have an abortion, so she needed to give the baby up for adoption. However, they didn't want to go through legal channels."

"What are you saying?" Riesling bolted to an upright position.

"According to what little paperwork I have, Doctor Allison helped facilitate a private illegal adoption right here in Candlewood Falls."

"You've got to be shitting me."

"I've got a letter from this doctor on winery stationery to my dad's friend, who wants to continue to remain anonymous, but his daughter wants to find her birth parents—"

"Can I see this letter?"

"I can show you a copy with the name blacked out. I promised my father's buddy I would keep his identity a secret. He might be old, but he's still relevant and you'd know him. He's kind of a household name."

"That's fine," Riesling said. "My mother was an only child. There was a lot of pressure on her because there was no one else to leave the winery to. Where my grandpa was the oldest of five. That said, my grandfather's siblings knew they wouldn't even be given the chance because it always went to the oldest. That was tradition."

"But you and your siblings don't seem to respond the same way."

"We all get a piece of the winery. My mom did the right thing and broke that bullshit, though she still managed to drive all her kids away and put huge roadblocks in all her relationships. The worst being myself and Malbec, but my mom didn't want the winery to only go to Malbec, yet she does want him to run it. He is the most gifted. Well, him and his soon-to-be wife."

"I find your family fascinating."

"They are a novelty. They will wear off." She laughed. "However, your little mystery has me intrigued. Ever since we uncovered my great-grandfather stole the winery from Eliza Jane's great-grandfather, most of us are interested in finding out what other secrets are buried on this winery. Well, everyone except Chablis. She's not interested in finding or creating any more drama for this family and I can understand that."

"But you're willing to go digging?"

"It's not that I want to go looking for trouble for my family." She shrugged. "And I doubt this could cause any; however, it's better to know and be prepared than to be blindsided."

Trey couldn't agree more, and he hated that any of

this could cause Riesling and her little girl any grief. But he needed to know who his parents were and if they had willingly given him up for adoption, or if they had been pressured in any way.

Even if he hadn't, he needed to understand the process and why his birth family had chosen this path.

He understood why Greg Levine, a well-known national talk show host, had his twenty-one-year-old model-actress girlfriend give up their daughter in an illegal adoption. He didn't agree with it, but he understood. Having spoken to Greg and his ex-girlfriend from back in the day, Trey accepted their decision.

But he still needed answers for himself.

He needed to find the records.

If they still existed.

Anything to send him in the right direction.

"I'll be honest with you," Riesling said. "We've searched the area near the building the doctor rented years ago. We did it because of the stories we heard and we found nothing."

"You actually took a shovel to the ground?"

"No. But my parents had cleaned out the old overflow building when the doctor left town and my grandfather had dug up so much of this land no one thought it necessary, I guess." She leaned back and lifted her glass to her lips as she stared at the sky.

He did the same, enjoying the stars that dotted the darkness, making a blanket of speckled light. As a kid, he used to love to stand on the balcony and look at the night sky and count the stars. He always wondered what would happen if they simply started falling from the sky. He imagined this array of gold lights hurling toward earth like a million sparklers on the Fourth of July.

"When my grandfather died, he did so with a fractured mind and he said some crazy shit. One of those things was this box of secrets buried by the river's edge. There are two buildings next to the river. One is where Malbec and Eliza Jane are living until their house is finished being built up on the hill behind the winery and the second is the overflow building where the doctor's office used to be. When I was a very small child, I do remember hearing my dad and mom argue with my grandpa about going out late at night on his treasure hunts. He'd lost his mind by then and he died a few years after Zinfandel was born, but I remember him talking gibberish about the secrets this place had if he could only unearth them."

"Where did he live at the end of his life?"

"My parents took care of him until the twins were born, and then he went into a nursing home."

"Weren't your folks divorced after you?"

She burst out laughing. "Yeah. They might be on paper and they don't live together, but they are one hundred percent a couple. More married than most. It's weird. Can't explain it and I won't try."

Trey held up one hand palm forward. "Not going to ask for further explanation." He polished off his wine and glanced at his watch. As much as he wanted to sit here all night and ask probing questions, it was time to go. His first patient was going to be banging on his door at seven thirty in the morning and they had a full day between that and working on finding a nurse and developing a new plan for clinic hours. If he was going to do this without using his trust or calling daddy, he needed to make more.

A lot more.

But he still needed to develop a plan for finding his birth parents. "So, how do you suggest I go about helping my friend find her birth parents?"

Riesling turned. "Have you been able to go through all the past records that Doctor Harden left?"

"Not even close."

"We start there. They needed to be purged anyway. We pull anyone who was seen by Doctor Allison. And I'll take you on a personal tour of the winery." She waggled her finger. "But there will be no digging. My mom wouldn't appreciate that. If we find something strange in our files here, we can take it to my dad. He's a wee bit more reasonable."

"Sounds fair enough." Trey knew he wouldn't be able to find an answer in a few weeks. Probably not even in a couple of months. He was going to have to be patient. "Thank you for helping me with this."

"We've all wondered why Doctor Allison maintained an office on our property when he examined patients right here."

"Wait. What?" Trey leaned forward. "You mean he used my office building?"

She nodded. "Harden is a second-generation doctor. He was originally in practice with his father who died of a heart attack fifteen years ago. William Harden, the dad, was closer in age with Doctor Allison. But back then, this was the only doctor in town outside of a midwife in Candlewood Falls. Otherwise, you had to go to the next town over. Now we've got a few ob-gyns to choose from."

"But only two general doctors and one of them is a hell of a lot farther out of town than I am."

She nodded. "And they don't have me."

"No, they don't." He stood, trying desperately not to smile. It wasn't that he didn't want her to see that he appreciated her in every way that counted. His concern was that he'd developed a deep attraction for Riesling and that scared him, not just because she was going to be angry that he hadn't been honest.

But because he was going to have to walk away from her and her adorable daughter.

"Thanks for a lovely day and evening. I really had a great time."

"So did I and trust me, I had my reservations."

He jerked his head. "Ouch. That hurt."

"Sorry. That didn't quite come out right." She took the hand he offered and rose gracefully from the chair.

His fingers remained tightly wrapped around hers as the warmth from her skin climbed across his, coating his body like a fleece blanket on a cold winter's night. Allowing himself to have any feelings for her was a mistake. It wouldn't help him find his birth parents. If anything, it would distract him from his goals. It was hard enough that he'd given up a lucrative practice and moved to nowhere New Jersey.

He didn't need any complications.

Yet, there he stood, staring into her sweet blue eyes, pulling her closer with the intention of kissing her and he wasn't sure he could stop. Not unless she shoved him away.

Her lips parted slightly as if to invite him in.

Inwardly he groaned. Outwardly he wrapped his arms around her waist and heaved her to his chest as he gently took her mouth in a passionate kiss. Their tongues twisted and twirled as if they were old lovers reunited after being apart for years.

She rested her hands on his shoulders, gliding them up his neck, massaging gently, driving him mad with desire.

"Wow," he whispered, taking a step back. "That was amazing, but we probably shouldn't have done that."

"Regret it already, do you?" She tucked her hair behind her ears.

"No. I didn't say that. I'm just considering our working relationship."

She patted his chest. "It's the wine. I'm a lightweight. So, no worries. Walk home safely. I'll see you in the morning."

Trey took her hand and kissed the palm. "Sleep well." He jogged down the steps and strolled toward the dirt road, not looking over his shoulder. While he didn't believe a word about her not being able to handle her booze, he was going to allow the white lie. He'd made the mistake by kissing her in the first place and she'd been gracious enough to give them both the out.

He needed to be a gentleman and take it.

It's what was best because when she found out he wasn't really looking for his friend, but for himself, she wasn't going to be mad; she was going to be furious, and he might as well not even bother unpacking.

7

CARTER

"Thanks for agreeing to see me." Carter fiddled with the tall paper mug and stared at the dark brew, enjoying the fresh pumpkin smell. When Green Bean started all these fancy coffees, he didn't think he'd like them, but his wife got him hooked and now he wasn't sure he even liked black anymore.

"It's been a long time," Harry said.

Carter never liked doing business the old-fashioned way, so anytime he had a chance to have a chat with someone anywhere outside of a stuffy office, he did it.

Of course, this wasn't really business. It was personal.

For both of them.

"How have you been?" Carter leaned back in his chair and glanced around the coffeehouse. It was later in the day, so not too many people milled about, which was a good thing. Not that Harry and Carter didn't meet every so often for a cup of Joe, but whenever they did, people wondered if that meant Theo was coming back to town.

"Doing as well as these old bones will let me." Harry smiled, raising his cup. "I'm going to be sixty-four this year."

"You've got a couple of years on me, old man." Carter laughed, tapping his mug against Harry's. "How's Cindy doing?"

"Oh, she's great." Harry beamed like a proud father should. His daughter lived a few towns over and had two kids. She was married to a lawyer and a good one, which Carter didn't say often about his own kind since most were out for their own interests and that didn't always match up with the clients. "The grandkids are wonderful. Growing too fast though. My wife is there this week helping out because George has a trial. I would have gone, but that brings us to why I called this meeting."

"Theo," Carter said, cutting to the chase. "Did he really book a flight to New Jersey?"

"That's what he told me and I reminded him he's not welcome here and not just in my house, but in Candlewood Falls."

"I know he's your son and I'm sorry to say this, but I hate that my daughter has to give him any information about where she lives. I resent he has any visitation at all."

"You don't have to apologize to me," Harry said. "I

stopped calling that boy my son a long time ago. If he shows up at my door, he'll be turned away."

"Why do you think he's coming? Is it because my girl and Ashling moved back?"

"We both know he don't care that much about anyone but himself," Harry said. "I've made a few calls and from what I've gathered, Theo has gotten himself into another scam much like the one that got him into trouble here."

"Wonderful," Carter muttered.

"So far, it looks legit. But I know it's not. Or if it is, Theo will manage to fuck it up or steal from the funds he's collecting."

"Sounds about right. So, why is he coming here?" Carter palmed his coffee, careful not to squeeze, even though the anger flowing through his veins burned hot. "Because the last time he saw Riesling, she tried to buy him off herself. We both know that didn't work."

Harry arched a brow. "She told you?"

Carter shook his head. "She's borrowed a little bit of money from Malbec and Chablis, but she acts as though I have no idea she's completely and utterly broke."

"When she moved back, we insisted on helping out with some things for Ashling. Your daughter wasn't thrilled with that, but in the end, she took our gifts."

"Thank you. I appreciate that." Carter was grateful that Harry had helped his daughter and grandchild. No matter how proud Carter was, he wouldn't deny Harry that privilege.

"We love that little girl." Harry smiled wide.

It warmed Carter's heart. He had only the one grandbaby, for now. He hoped to have many more. "She's a chip off the old block."

Harry nodded. "But what are we going to do about Theo?"

Carter lifted his briefcase off the chair next to him and took out some papers. "I have Weezer's blessing on this one, so you don't have to worry about her."

"I used to be afraid of Weezer until I got to know her."

"She's a good woman. Misunderstood, but she's got a heart of gold." Carter pushed the documents across the table. "Theo is driven by money and the perception of power. I say perception because he doesn't understand how to get power or how to maintain it, much less what it means. He lacks the fundamental concept that it's not all about fear, but more about respect. He also doesn't get that if he wants both, he needs to have trust first, and that train left the building a long time ago."

"Theo has always wanted things the quick and easy way."

"There's no such thing, but you and I know that." Harry lifted the papers. "What are these?"

"Parental termination."

Harry glanced over the top. "Does Riesling know about this?"

"She knows I drew them up, but she doesn't know I plan on coming after Theo. If she did, she'd tell me not to."

"I've never known you to play this hard." Harry lifted his mug and took a long sip. "Not even when she followed Theo; you let her walk."

"Because I thought she'd come running home with her tail between her legs after the baby was born. I was wrong. Since then, I've respected my daughter's wishes because I will not let her walk out of my life again." Carter raised his index finger. "However, when I found out she gave him all her money to try to get rid of him, well, that changed everything. I just wished he'd stayed away, but it looks like that's not the case."

Harry set the legal documents down and ran a hand across his face. "If Theo is involved in another pyramid-type scheme, I want to nail his ass and send him to prison. Do you think that's possible?"

Carter had thought about that too. A lot. "My first priority is to make sure he has no claim to Ashling. My daughter has a heart of gold and she doesn't want to be the kind of mother that poisons her child against their father. She's like that in part because of the way Weezer and I divorced and in part because she's seen firsthand with some friends how cruel parents can get with the things they say."

"Ashling is a smart young girl," Harry said. "Do you

know when she's with me she never asks about Theo. I take that back. She once asked me if he was coming to visit. When I told her no, she had this major look of relief on her face and the rest of the day was filled with laughter. She had so much fun she begged Riesling to spend the night. She even told her mom that it would be *safe*. Interesting word, right?"

Carter had to agree about the word choice. He glanced toward the ceiling. Riesling and his grandbaby had been living in Candlewood Falls now for about a month and during that time he didn't think Ashling had asked about her dad a single time. Most kids talked about their parents.

And Ashling talked about her mother all the time when Riesling wasn't around.

But never Theo.

Until Theo came to town and then it's all the little girl could think about. However, when he left, she would cry for days. Mostly because he would leave without saying goodbye, or break a date they had, or he couldn't tell her when he'd be back.

It would take a good two weeks before Ashling would bounce back to her normal spunky self and this was a cycle Carter never wanted to see his grandbaby go through again.

Ever.

He shifted his gaze and blew out a slow breath. "Do you have information that he's involved in something?"

Harry glanced over his shoulder as if he were

nervous about something and then lifted his cell from the table. "It turns out Theo might have actually grown a brain, but not really." He slid his phone across the table. "Five months ago, he filed for incorporation. The name of his company is TNT Enterprise. It's really a pyramid scheme, from what I can tell and he's only the front man."

"How do you know all this?" Carter scanned the information on the screen, picking up the key information. While the words were powerful and interesting, he'd rather hear the summation from Harry.

"When I heard Riesling tried to pay him off, I'd had enough. I know her well enough that if she knew I got too deep, she'd cut me off at the knees. So, I decided to hire a private investigator."

"Shit," Carter mumbled. "I've got one too. We need to coordinate efforts. We can't have our people stumbling over each other."

"Easily done."

"Since your guy has found more than mine, we'll go with yours," Carter said. "Or they can work together."

"Let's have them meet and we can go from there."

Carter nodded. "Tell me more about what you found out." He downed the last of his coffee, which had gotten cold, but he didn't care. He set the cell on the table and leaned back, folding his arms, doing his best to keep his anger in check. Being emotional wasn't going to do him any good. Right now, he needed to keep a level head.

"This company, from the outside, appears to be a multilevel marketing corporation." Harry held up his hand when Carter opened his mouth to interject. "The products are all geared to men. It's a manscaping grooming line. But it's also a wellness program and that's the upsell. They get men to join. They aren't required to carry a lot of product, but there is an initial investment. From there, you get bonus points for growing your business. The bigger your store, the more money you can make. There is a real push to buy product in bulk. And there is a bigger push to get your team to do the same. The more your team sells, which really means buys, the more you make. And then there are the wellness classes, which you sell to your team and to your clients."

"My head hurts just listening to that." Carter leaned forward and rubbed his temples. "The Federal Trade Commission hasn't come down on them?"

"It's a new company and there hasn't been a formal complaint, yet," Harry said. "My guy, Brian, said there are two men who are starting to bitch, but they are being told to be patient. That it takes time to grow this kind of business and that they will see the results in a few months. Brian told me that after that, Theo and his partner, Stu, gave those two men bonus points to be collected when they hit a certain level. I guess those are worth money."

"If he's only been at this for five months, he couldn't have collected that much money," Carter said.

"The buy-in for the platinum level is ten grand. They have two hundred men at that level and six hundred have joined to date."

"Jesus. He's been hustling," Carter said. "Where did he get the start-up cash?"

"His partner developed the product. From what I've ascertained, he put his life savings into it and is now scrambling to make it work and this was his way of feeding the beast."

"He sounds more desperate than anything else." Carter took his legal documents and placed them neatly back in his briefcase. "And we've got our work cut out for us."

"I'd appreciate it if you didn't say anything to my wife about this. She's still holding out hope her boy will change."

Carter nodded. "I believe it's best if this stays between us. Even though Weezer knows exactly what I'm up to, she doesn't want to know."

Harry tilted his head. "That doesn't sound like Weezer."

"Part of her is tired of the burden of secrets, but she can't be the one who does any of this or Riesling will hate her. I'd rather take the wrath of Riesling than have to listen to my wife cry over it anymore."

"I hear you on that." Harry stood, taking both empty coffee paper mugs. "Keep in touch."

"You do the same." Carter leaned back and sighed.

After that conversation he could use a stiff drink. He glanced at his watch. It was pushing five. He could stop at the local bar for one drink before heading home. Besides, Weezer had her weekly bunco group tonight and wouldn't be home—if she came over—until after nine.

He was going to have to remedy their living situation soon. He'd hoped Malbec would want to live in his childhood house, but he and Eliza Jane had opted to build a new place on the property.

That made sense.

But Carter was tired of living partially separate lives. He and Weezer belonged together.

Under the same roof.

Trey

"Hey, Koontz. How are you feeling today?" Trey set his medical tablet on the counter, rolled up his sleeves, and washed his hands.

"Pretty good. I'm still run-down a bit, but better."

"That's good." Trey pulled his stethoscope off his neck and listened to Koontz's heart. It sounded strong. "Have you given any more thought to my recommendation for Ella?" He continued with his exam, checking all of the old man's vitals. So far, Koontz was in good shape, for a man in his nineties. Actually, considering he'd suffered a mild heart attack, he was better off than some men half his age.

But life was quickly catching up him and he could no longer take care of his daughter, much less himself.

"Son. How long have you lived here?"

"Not very long," Trey admitted. However, he didn't want to bring up Theo or the fact that Koontz had lost a fair amount of money when he'd invested Riesling's ex. That would be rude. "Why?"

"If you'd been part of this town longer, you'd know that I don't have the kind of money to pay for a facility like that for my girl. Or for me."

"That's not the option I was talking about." Trey set his equipment down and quickly picked up his tablet, recording all the necessary information before he pulled up his chair. "You both qualify for home health care. It's limited, but we can set up someone to come out to the house every day." Trey had made sure he'd gotten confirmation from the insurance company before he even looked into any programs. He didn't want to get the old man's hopes up. "There's also an adult day care that I looked into that she could go to two days a week. It would be good for her to be around other patients like her and it would give you some time to yourself and to rest. You need it."

Koontz let out a long breath. "That all sounds great, but what happens when I die?" He blinked. "And that's going to happen probably long before she does. What then? Who is going to look after my girl then?"

That was a valid question. One that he didn't have an answer for yet.

This wasn't where he'd planned on living out his days. It was bad enough he'd already decided on investing in a clinic, but that was because it was the right thing to do for the community and it would make the sale of his practice all the more enticing. Especially when everyone was going to ask why he didn't stick around very long.

He almost laughed out loud. If he found the answers he was looking for, everyone would know anyway.

"And I don't want her going into some state-run place. I've seen them," Koontz said as his eyes filled with tears.

"While there are some excellent state-run homes, I understand your concern."

Koontz shook his head. "No. You don't. You see I had the money and I had her name on a waiting list at Bedford. But then I listened to someone I shouldn't have and now that bed is gone and so is the money."

At least the old man didn't blame Riesling.

"I'm told Ella could live for another ten years like this. We both know I'm not lasting that long."

Trey had to agree. But he wasn't about to say that out loud. "There are a lot of work-arounds," Trey said. "For now, would you be willing to look into these other options? Let's maximize your benefits for the rest of this year and I will look at some affordable long-term care options."

"That's not your job, Doc."

"Are you and Ella my patients?"

Koontz nodded.

"Then it's all part of the deal in my practice," he said. Now all he had to do was muster up the courage to ask about Doctor Allison. Thus far, no natural progression of conversation led itself into that topic.

"You're one of a kind."

"That's what my mom always said."

Koontz tilted his head. "You say that as though she's no longer with us."

"She passed a few years ago."

"I'm so sorry for your loss." Koontz buttoned up his shirt with a shaky hand.

"Thank you." It was now or wait a few weeks. "Do you mind if I ask you something?"

"Sure. Go ahead."

Trey felt more comfortable if he stood for this part of the discussion. "What can you tell me about Doctor Robert Allison? He was listed as the ob-gyn who delivered Ella, as well as being Ella's doctor. Also, as I clean out some of the files in the office, I'm finding his name on a lot of records. I just find it weird he kept an office on The River Winery."

"My wife and Ella only saw him at this office, so I wouldn't know anything about that," Koontz said. "He was a good man. Well-liked by everyone in town. We all tried to get him to make Candlewood Falls his main practice, but he never did. He came here once or twice a week, though sometimes more because he did take on a few high-risk pregnancies."

That was news to Trey since not one file he'd pulled was anything other than a normal full-term birth. "It sounds like you knew him well."

"I wouldn't go that far, but we played a round or two of golf every year." Koontz laughed. "That man loved the sport, but he sucked. I mean he was horrible at golf. I hated taking him out to my club, but he belonged to a top fifty course about sixty miles from here and if I took him to mine, he'd reciprocate."

"That makes sense."

"Why do you want to know about Allison? He's long since passed."

That was a good question and one Trey wasn't sure he should be honest about, but hadn't really come up with a good lie, so he decided to come close to the truth. Always better that way. "I came across an adoption record that has some abnormalities to it and the doctor on record is Allison."

"I see." Koontz ran a hand across his mouth. "Is this someone you know personally? Or is it random?"

Now that as an interesting question. "It's personal."

"Doctor Allison didn't have a regular office anywhere. He spent a couple of days here. A couple of days somewhere else and his office stationery never matched that of the office he practiced out of. Don't you find that strange?" Koontz asked. "Because I always did."

"I don't know anything about his other offices." Trey leaned against the counter and folded his arms. "What can you tell me?"

"Only my suspicions."

"I'm listening." Trey's pulse soared. This felt like the first real possible clue and even though he felt guilty for using Koontz this way, he'd pay the old man back in spades.

"I do believe that Allison was a good doctor and gave my bride the best care possible. I have no complaints about that. However, I overheard someone talking in the locker room of his country club that for the right price, Allison could help solve this man and his mistress's problem. This was forty years ago, so it wasn't an abortion they were talking about since those were legal."

"Black market adoptions?" Trey tossed out there with a thick tongue.

"That's my assumption, but I never dug any deeper. He was never accused of anything. I don't believe anyone ever complained about him and that's the only time I've ever heard that, until you brought it up."

Slowly, Koontz slipped off the exam table. "I honestly don't know any more and I should get going. I'm sure Riesling has had enough of my Ella."

"I appreciate you being so candid with me." Trey opened the exam room door and led Koontz out to the lobby where his daughter sat with Riesling.

Ella glanced up and smiled. She still knew who her father was, at least most days. And she often recognized Riesling as someone she was supposed to know, but for the most part, her mind was gone and that broke Trey's heart.

"Koontz is going to go ahead and sign up for what we talked about," Trey said to Riesling.

"Wonderful. I'll file the paperwork. If all goes as planned, this can start as early as next week." Riesling helped Ella to her feet.

"That fast?" Koontz asked.

Trey nodded. "Enjoy your Thanksgiving. Make sure you don't overdo it."

"Sure thing, Doc. Thanks again."

Riesling held the door open. Once they were safely outside, she turned and stared at him with a questioning glare.

"What?"

"You know his insurance won't cover all that," she said as she pulled the door closed.

He shrugged. "I'll cover the cost of the adult day care. It's not that much. He's going to end up having a stroke if he doesn't start slowing down."

"And where are you going to get the—"

"That's none of your business."

Riesling didn't need to know he was a spoiled rich kid. Well, he was a grown-ass adult with a father who had boatloads of money to which he would inherit someday. Actually, he had a fucking incredibly large bank account that he refused to do anything with because he wanted to make it on his own.

Well, this had nothing to do with that and so what if he dipped into the money his father gave him in order to help out an old man and his sick aging daughter?

"I'm all for helping them out and I think that's really sweet of you, but will that affect hiring a nurse and opening up clinic hours?"

He shook his head. "I've got the money for that too."

"How? Where?"

He waggled his finger. "It's all part of my business plan and all approved by the powers that be."

"And exactly who or what are those powers?" She planted her hands on her hips and glared.

God. She was so adorable when she got feisty and inquisitive at the same time.

"I have some money saved and this is where I want to spend it. There's nothing for you to worry about." He closed the gap. "That was our last patient for the day. Do you have to race home or go pick up Ashling?"

"She's staying with my parents."

He circled his arms around Riesling's waist and tugged her to his chest. The last time they had kissed, she'd blamed it on alcohol. He, of course, had been the one who'd decided it shouldn't have happened and yet, it was all he could think about since. "What are you doing for dinner?"

"Not much. Tomorrow is Thanksgiving and I'm saving my stomach for all the horrible things I'm going to put in it."

He laughed. "I totally forgot tomorrow was a holiday."

"You're not going home to see your dad?"

"Not this year." He gently tucked a piece of her hair behind her ear. "It's going to be impossible to keep this strictly personal."

"We really should."

"You're not making it any easier when you press your breasts against my chest, massage my shoulders, and lick your lips like that."

"I'm thinking about eating turkey," she whispered.

That statement should have made him laugh, but he was hyperfocused on her mouth. And kissing it. Which he did. The kiss was soft. Sweet. Tender. And lingered for a good five minutes. He could have stood there and kissed her all night. He certainly wanted to, only his damn phone went off.

"Sorry." He pulled it from his pocket. "That's my dad and he wants to FaceTime," he said. "Can you give me a—"

She leaned in and kissed his cheek. "I should go. I have things to do before tomorrow. We'll catch up on Friday."

He nodded and watched her waltz out the door. It had been a long time since he'd felt this out of control about his feelings toward a woman and he needed to rein them in.

8

RIESLING

The closer it got to Thanksgiving, the more Riesling wanted to get the hell out of Candlewood Falls.

Having a holiday dinner with her family, when everyone was actually home, while always entertaining and full of laughs, also ended up being stressful and someone inevitably got into it with Weezer.

For years it was almost always Malbec, when he came home. Or often Merlot because of Racheal. Sometimes it was Chablis because she'd bring a date to deflect when she'd been told she couldn't bring a random man unless the family had met him before.

That had always been the rule.

Chablis wasn't one to follow the rules. Not since she'd gone all the way through college, getting the degree that had been expected of her and then finding out Malbec had no intention of running the winery with her. That's when she decided doing what had been expected wasn't ever going to be in the plans again.

Until Malbec moved home.

That changed everything.

For everyone.

But she also didn't know what to do about Trey, or the way he made her feel, or the fact that every time he brought his lips to her mouth she could no longer think straight.

That was a feeling she never thought she'd want to welcome after what had happened with Theo, yet she enjoyed Trey so much that losing herself for a few moments with him almost seemed like a reasonable thing to do.

And he wasn't Theo.

He was a well-educated, successful doctor who had a fucking heart. She clutched her chest. Who the hell spent their own money to help out an old man and their daughter? No doctor ever did that. At least not one she'd ever worked with and yet, Trey was about to dish out a decent chunk of change to cover what insurance wouldn't so Koontz could have about ten hours to himself every week.

Trey made her question her desire to remain single, which was shocking all by itself. She hadn't really dated in years, and not because she'd been heartbroken over Theo. Her reason for not wanting a man in her life had more to do with Ashling becoming attached and then having her little heart torn to pieces again and that was something Riesling wasn't willing to put on the line for anyone.

The timer dinged, pulling Riesling from her thoughts. She set her book down, which she realized she'd turned five pages, but couldn't remember a single thing about what had graced her eyes. She stood, stretched, and padded toward the kitchen.

She couldn't believe tomorrow was Thanksgiving. It seemed like just yesterday it was Halloween. She inhaled sharply.

What the hell? Why didn't her kitchen smell like melting apples and cinnamon? She yanked open the oven. "Shit," she mumbled. She'd done it again. "I suck at baking. Hell. I suck at cooking." She wondered if she could leave the apple crumble in the oven while it preheated.

Probably not.

She sighed as she pulled it out and turned the dial. It was a little after eleven and she had to be up at six. It would take five to ten minutes for the oven to heat to the right temperature, and then another forty minutes to cook.

Her cell phone buzzed. She jumped. Reaching for it, her heart plummeted to the bottom of her gut. Ashling was spending the night with her parents, which she did often, so there wasn't generally a reason to worry. But when her phone went off after bedtime, it always made Riesling freak out.

The last time Ashling needed her in the middle of

the night, it had been because Theo called her and if that were the case, right before Thanksgiving, Riesling was going to lose her shit.

Trey: *If you're awake, turn on the news. You're going to want to see this.*

She read the text twice before picking up the remote to the small television she'd hung in the corner of the kitchen. She pointed it, clicked, and gasped as she stared at a picture of Theo.

"What the fuck?" She turned up the volume.

"Theo Richardson and his partner, Stu Uberlacker, are under investigation for running a pyramid scheme. Their company, TNT Enterprise, is a male wellness and grooming business that appears to be more product oriented, but the FTC is looking into allegations that those who buy into the system make their money by encouraging more to buy into the company, not by selling products and services. Both Theo and Stu have made official statements and are cooperating. They have stated that the allegations are unfounded."

She turned the television off and pulled down a bottle of red wine and poured a full glass. She took three good gulps before picking up her cell.

Riesling: *Thanks for the heads-up.*

Trey: *I'm outside. Want company?*

Her heart jumped to her throat. She tried to swallow but her muscles didn't want to work. She turned on her heel. Careful not to spill, she carried her wine to the door and opened it. "Why are you here?" She hadn't meant to sound so rude, but the moment she'd seen the story on the TV, her mood had completely soured.

"As soon as I saw the headlines, I pulled it up on my tablet and jogged over to make sure you were okay." He held up something in his hand. The news was still playing on the screen. "I was worried about you, especially being out here all alone."

"You didn't have to do that." She held up her glass. "But since you're here and I'm going to be up for the next hour waiting for the crumble to finish, would you like to come in and join me?"

"Wine sounds awesome, but why are you still baking so late?"

"That's a loaded question," she said with a flip of her free hand. "One I'm not willing to answer for fear you might tease me."

"Why, I would never." He followed her into the house.

"Make yourself at home." Her cell buzzed.

And buzzed.

And buzzed again.

All texts from her family. It was late, and all the messages were regarding the news program. If she ignored her family, they would get the hint that she had no desire to deal with this news right now.

Only now Malbec was calling.

She sent it right to voicemail before pouring a very large glass of vino for her houseguest. She touched her lips, remembering the kiss from earlier. Trey certainly knew his way around her lips. She wouldn't stop him if he tried to kiss her again. Hell, she'd consider initiating it herself if the right opportunity found itself, though tonight might not be the right set of circumstances.

She carried both glasses back into the family room and handed him one.

He'd opted to sit on the sofa, which she thought was interesting. She could either sit with him or across the room in the recliner. She chose the former.

"I take it you had no idea about your ex and the investigation into his company." Trey stretched out his free arm over the back of the couch.

"I haven't spoken to Theo in three months. That was the last time he called our daughter."

"Jerk," Trey mumbled. "I don't pretend to know what it's like to be a father, but I can't imagine going more than a few days without speaking to my kid."

"Trust me, it's torture." She'd never gone more than a week, and those seven days had been the hardest time of her life. She never wanted to do it again. "I always answer the phone when he calls because I know Ashling wants to hear from her father."

"Are you sure about that?"

She opened her mouth, but nothing happened. No words formed. No sound came out. She cleared her throat. "Why would you ask me that?"

"You're assuming that Ashling wants a relationship with a man she barely knows just because he's her father. But does she beg to see him or call him?"

"No. However, whenever Theo ends a visit, she cries for days. That tells me all I need." Not that she needed to explain all this to Trey, but maybe she needed to remind herself. "Besides, Theo has visitation. I can't deny him his child. If I did, he could take me to court."

"I understand, but have you ever tried to—"

"You sound like my mother." She raised her very full glass of wine to her mouth and chugged half of it. God, her family knew how to make a good wine. Even when she chose not to sip it like it was meant to be drank. She set her glass aside. She didn't need to be hungover for Thanksgiving dinner, especially when she'll be fielding off questions. Of course she didn't have any answers. "You don't know the kind of person Theo is or how he can make my life miserable. I do the best I can with what I've been dealt."

"I'm not judging you."

"But you are trying to give me advice on how to handle someone you've never met."

"That is true," he admitted. "When I first went to medical school, I thought I wanted to be a psychiatrist, and sometimes I tend to fall back on that desire since I did pause medical school to get a master's degree in psychology." He had the nerve to shush her by holding up his hand. "I get I'm not a parent and this is none of my business. Only, I can tell you don't want him in your life or in Ashling's. So, why don't you do something about it?"

"Jesus. You don't think I've tried?" Tears burned the

corner of her eyes. A sudden tightness in her chest made it difficult to catch her breath. Even her family had stopped pushing her this hard when it came to Theo. No one wanted him around, but everyone, including her lawyer father and her meddling mother understood she had to respect the visitation agreement.

The one time she hadn't, Theo had flexed his muscles and she spent an entire week wondering if she'd ever see her daughter again.

"It's not like I can just tell him he can't see her. It doesn't work that way. He took me to court. He was granted visitation rights and I have to let him see her when he wants to exercise those rights."

"But it sounds like to me, he doesn't follow the rules and maybe you could get a judge to see what a deadbeat father he is."

She blew out puff of air, dropped her head back, and closed her eyes. No one got it except her parents and they didn't want to accept it. They honestly believed taking Theo to court again would be beneficial when all it would do was give him a reason to make her life miserable. He would tell the judge that he was working hard to change his life and working a million different jobs. He'd cry some sob story on how it was hard to find time off to get to New Jersey to see his little girl. And the hardest part was that getting the case in front of a judge was damn near impossible. He didn't owe her money because he didn't have any to sue for child support and they'd never been married so there was no alimony to be had. "Theo doesn't have custody. I do. All he has is visitation. He isn't required to pay me a dime because he doesn't have any and honestly, I don't want his money if he were to all of a sudden come into it. That would just give him the kind of leverage over me I don't want him to have."

"Then why are you playing this game with him?"

"Because I don't have a choice." She blinked open her eyes and glared. "If I deny him a visit, he can come after me for breaking a court order. And he's done it. I won't go through that again. I won't put my girl through that." She swiped at the tears burning a path down her cheeks. "As long as Theo is in his own world doing his own thing, we're safe."

"Until he gets himself into financial trouble. Then he comes knocking down your door."

"The well's dry. There's nothing left," she mumbled as she reached for her drink. Before she could bring it to her lips, Trey snatched it right from her fingertips.

"That's not going to help."

"It's not going to hurt."

"I beg to differ." He took both glasses and brought them into the kitchen.

She could hear him rustling through the cupboards. She should be insulted, and maybe she was, but she didn't have the energy to care. Theo had gotten himself into some serious financial trouble and that meant he'd be knocking on her door right quick. Theo had taken every penny she'd saved over the years and her parents wouldn't give her a dime.

Not that she'd ask. She'd never put her folks in that position.

Trey strolled back into the family room carrying a mug of hot tea and some warm apple crumble.

She scowled. "That was for tomorrow. My mom was expecting me to make dessert."

"I've got more apples. I'll make another batch before you have to leave in the morning." He disappeared into the kitchen only to return with another cup of tea and some more of her decadent dish. "If it's not ready by the time you need to leave, I'll drive it over."

"It doesn't matter." She took a big bite and groaned. It was actually good, and she'd made it herself. Too bad her family wasn't going to get a chance to taste it. "My mom will have a backup apple something or other. It's not that she didn't trust that I wouldn't attempt to make something. It's just that I suck that bad in the kitchen."

"Don't worry. I'll make sure you have something amazing to bring tomorrow."

She shoveled half the delicious treat into her mouth before washing it down with some tea. "What are you doing tomorrow?"

"I'm going to continue to go through all the old files that Doctor Harden left behind and enter them into an electronic database while I look for other patients of

Doctor Allison's, hoping to find clues regarding my friend's adoption."

"I did look at that letter." She wished she hadn't tucked it in the top drawer in her desk upstairs. "It didn't really tell me anything. Would it be okay with you if I showed my parents?"

"Let me ask you this." Trey set his empty plate on the coffee table and shifted closer. "Do you think it's possible Doctor Allison could have been running a black market adoption ring?"

"Not much gets past my mom in this town, but that was a long time ago, so maybe."

"Would she keep it a secret?"

Riesling laughed. "My mother has a reputation for being a gossip, which is exactly the opposite of what she is, though she is a busybody and a know-it-all. However, she doesn't repeat things unless they are absolutely true and even then, it's not like she spreads things around like wildfire."

"Do you ever answer a question with a simple yes or no?"

"What you asked isn't simple." Riesling rested her head on her arm. Her mother was tough to explain, even to those who knew her, so to have to try to give Trey the lowdown seemed impossible. "My mom will repeat something if she believes it's necessary. She will keep your secrets but not your lies and transgressions, if that makes any sense."

"But she lied about the ownership of the winery."

"In the end she did what was right and at a huge cost to her personally." It was rare that Riesling defended her mother. Especially in regard to her decision to continue to lie about who actually owned the winery or how the River family came to own it themselves. But that was all in the past now. "Like I said, your question was not a yes or no answer."

"So you don't believe that if Doctor Allison was running an illegal adoption ring out of Candlewood Falls and anyone in your family knew about it, he'd be able to get away with it."

"Is that what you really think he was doing?" Riesling sat up taller. Her grandfather had told stories about the doctor hiding something but everyone, including her mother, had thought Grandpa had lost his mind. "Because your piece of paper isn't any indication of that."

"No. It's not. But my friend's adoption has a lot of question marks. Her birth records were forged and—"

She dropped her chin to her chest. "You failed to mention that juicy piece of information."

"I know. I'm sorry. I'm trying to be discreet. I'm not here to hurt anyone and since Doctor Allison is dead, it's not like the authorities will be bringing charges or anything."

"No. But there might still be accomplices. Are you willing to share the records with me?" Riesling reached out and wrapped her fingers around his forearm. "I'm happy to help you solve this mystery. I understand wanting to know where you came from and if the adoption wasn't on the up and up, then it shouldn't be too hard to figure out."

"It was thirty-five years ago. Nothing was digital. It was easier to hide a paper trail back then."

"Easier, but still pretty hard," she said. "Why don't you bring me everything you have tomorrow. We should be—better yet—why don't you come to Thanksgiving dinner. My family won't mind."

"I don't want to impose."

"You won't be. If my mom knew you were going to be spending Thanksgiving alone, without any family, she'd be hog-tying you and dragging your ass to her home for a feast River style."

Trey palmed her cheek. "You're impossible to say no to." He lowered his chin. "On both accounts." He brushed his thumb across her lips.

Butterflies filled her gut as he leaned closer.

"But I'm only going to go if you want me to."

"I do," she whispered. It was an honest answer. Maybe too honest. Since she'd met Trey, he'd been all she could think about. He'd made coming home more than a soft place to land.

He made her feel as though for the first time in a long time she'd made the right decision. It wasn't just that he valued her as a physician's assistant, because any good doctor could do that. Hell, the last one she'd worked for had created an atmosphere that she thrived in, and Trey had done exactly the same thing, except he took it to a new level. He trusted her with every aspect of his practice. That was something even her last employer hadn't done.

"You should tell me to leave." He twisted a piece of her hair between his finger and thumb. "Otherwise, I might try to kiss you and more."

Getting tangled up with her boss was a horrible idea. Only, staring into his chocolate eyes, there was no way she was sending him back out into the cold. Not tonight. She stood and lifted her shirt over her head before shimmying out of her sweatpants. She stood before him in just her sports bra and boy shorts. "I'm going to head upstairs. You can join me for the kissing and more, or you can let yourself out. The choice is yours." She turned on her heel and didn't glance over her shoulder.

She didn't have to. She could feel the floorboards rattle as he followed her toward her bedroom.

Trey

Ever since Trey learned his adoption wasn't legal, he

hadn't had much time for dating. Even before that, he avoided relationships thanks to his ex-wife.

But Riesling was different.

She wasn't like most women he'd met over the years. She had this incredible personality, when she let it out, which wasn't often enough. And her heart was made with a combination of gold and sweet marshmallows, all warm and gooey.

He tugged at his shirt as he stepped into her room. A queen bed sat proudly between the two small windows overlooking the man-made pond that faced the old farmhouse. He couldn't see the structure, but the lights lining the dirt road filtered through the glass windowpane that was in much need of a cleaning. He kicked off his boots and unfastened his jeans while staring at her half-naked body sprawled out on the mattress.

She was perfect with her flawless skin and toned muscles. But what stole his breath was her genuine smile. He couldn't think straight half the time when he was in her presence. He tried to and mostly he faked it well, especially when he focused on finding out all the pieces to the puzzle of his adoption.

However, outside of that, all he wanted was this moment and now that he was in it, he was like a scared young man about to have sex for the first time.

At thirty-five.

Okay. Now he was being dramatic.

He slipped from his pants and climbed into bed, pulling her tight to his body. He stared into her eyes as he gently pressed his mouth on hers. The moment their lips touched, it was as if fireworks exploded on his tongue. If he'd wanted to take things slow, it was no longer possible. The heat between them had been turned up to incineration.

Her hands roamed his body as if she were an octopus with eight tentacles. Not that he was going to complain about her passion. However, he could barely catch his breath as he grappled with the few articles of clothing they had left between them.

She flipped him onto his back and straddled him.

He gripped her hips and sucked in a deep breath as she leaned over him, her perfect, round breasts only inches from his mouth.

Licking his lips, he lifted his head and sucked her nipple.

She moaned, arching her back.

Tonight would be an exercise in self-control, which he knew he'd lose, but he'd try to maintain it for as long as he could. He hadn't wanted a woman this badly in a long time. He couldn't remember the last girl that had this effect on him with the exception of his ex-wife and she no longer counted.

He turned her over and kissed every inch of her body. He didn't want to let a part of her go untouched.

She returned the favor and then some.

He nearly lost it when she curled her fingers around

his length and brought her lips to him, but he managed to keep it together, enjoying her firm but tender touch.

Generally, he was a selfish man in the bedroom, taking what he needed and desired. It wasn't that he didn't care about giving the woman he was with pleasure, but that was always the byproduct of their combined actions. However, his need to ensure her ultimate satisfaction overwhelmed and consumed him. It was all that mattered in the moment.

Gently, he pushed her from him and nestled himself between her legs, tasting her sweetness. It was like filling his mouth with forbidden fruit.

Her soft moans echoed in the night. They grew louder and stronger until she clutched his head, digging her fingers into his scalp.

"Trey," she whispered. "Yes."

He kissed his way to her lips, entering her slowly. Their tongues twisted and turned in the same dance as their bodies. It went from slow and romantic to fast, wild, and out of control. They each knew instinctively what the other wanted and when. Their lovemaking was instinctive and natural. It was as if he was meant to be with Riesling. As if there was no other woman who could ever understand him this way.

She convulsed underneath him, clutching at his body.

His climax tore through his system like a race car screaming around the track and crossing the finish line.

This was an unexpected complication. He tried to

catch his breath as he pulled the covers over their bodies.

She rested her head on his chest and he kissed her temple.

Trey was a grown man. He'd been married. Divorced. He was thirty-five and he'd had a string of dead-end relationships and that's the way he liked it. Women, once they found out how many zeroes were in his bank account, generally only wanted one thing: money.

Riesling didn't have two pennies to rub together, but Trey believed she was rich in other ways.

"Don't forget you promised to make more crumble," Riesling said as she snuggled closer. Her fingers flicked across his pectoral muscles.

He could get used to having her in his arms on a regular basis.

"My internal clock will have me up at five. That will give me plenty of time go back to my place and make your dessert."

"Thanks. We can drive to my folks' place together."

"I have to ask. When you say your parents' house, which one are you talking about?"

"Usually my mom's. That's the one that's been in our family for generations. My mom is a little upset that Malbec and Eliza Jane don't want to live there, but there are six more of us."

"Would you want to live there?"

"God, no. And not because I don't love that house. I

do. I also believe one of us should take it. However, it's just not for me."

"Where do you want to live? I mean, this can't be your dream home."

She let out a soft laugh. "The house my father's in."

9

RIESLING

Riesling gently shut Trey's passenger car door. "Internal clock my ass. Not only are we late, but we don't have a dish to pass."

"I'm not the one who woke me up at three in the morning for round two."

Her cheeks flushed. She hadn't spent the entire night with a man since she'd been with Theo. It was always too complicated because of Ashling.

"You could have just stayed up then."

Trey laughed. "You wore me out."

"My family is about to wear you down in a different way."

"I think I can handle them." He strolled around the hood of the car and stretched out his arm, curling his fingers through hers and tugging her toward the front porch.

She hesitated for a moment. "We're not supposed to bring—"

"There you two are." Her mother swung open the front door wearing her typical jeans and flannel shirt with her perfectly styled hair, and the makeup she'd applied looked as though it had been done by a professional.

There were moments in Riesling's life where she wished she could be more like her mother. More like her old authentic self. The person she used to be before Theo sucked the life out of her, taking from her more than all her money. That asshole had robbed her of her spirit and she hadn't figured out how to get it back.

"Happy turkey day," she said. "Sorry we're late." Did she just say *we're*? And her mother's not bellowing about someone coming to a family dinner that wasn't expressly invited by her, ahead of time.

"Not a problem. Your father didn't put the turkey in the oven when I asked him to, so dinner's going to be about half an hour later than expected." Her mother put her hands on her hips. "Where's this famous apple crumble I've been hearing about?"

Riesling's heart hit her gut like a ton of bricks. She resented that not being able to bring a simple dessert could bring shame to her soul in a matter of seconds.

"I ate it," Trey said with an amused tone. "I'm sorry. I didn't realize it was for today's feast, which is stupid, but when I went over to Riesling's last night after the news broke, I devoured half of it and I didn't have any apples to replace it."

Riesling swallowed. There was so much to read into that statement and while Trey had been standing right next to her when she'd spoken to Malbec about what happened with Theo and his new male wellness business, no one knew Trey had been with her last night because that wasn't her family's business.

"Well, that's all right. I've got a whole bushel of apples that Ashling and Carter picked yesterday. You and Riesling can use my kitchen. We can bake it after the turkey comes out; that way it will be nice and hot when it's time for dessert." Her mother looped her arm through Trey's. "I'm sure glad you could make it today." Her mother led the way up to the house. "Everyone is in the backyard. Trey, why don't you head outside. I need a moment with my girl."

"Yes, ma'am."

Here it comes. At least this time her mother opted to rip Riesling a new one in private instead of doing it in front of their company, which almost never happened. Normally, The Weezer enjoyed not only embarrassing her children, but whoever they brought home. Her philosophy, which Riesling's father often shared, was that if you couldn't handle being in the hot seat in the River family, then you couldn't handle being *in* the family.

Sometimes Riesling didn't believe she fit in any longer, thanks to Theo.

Merlot always told Riesling that it was in her head, much like how Chablis felt about her dreams being stolen from her fingertips because of Malbec's and their mother's feud.

Riesling watched as Trey disappeared out the back door. He glanced over his shoulder and gave her a slight smile.

It damn near melted her heart.

"Come here, sweetheart." Her mother pulled her into her arms and gave her the biggest bear hug. It was the kind of embrace that Riesling remembered when she'd been a small child and her mom would snuggle with her while reading a story. "How are you holding up?"

"I'm doing okay," she said with a slight tremor in her voice. "Ashling doesn't know anything, does she?"

"No. Grandpa has turned off the cable, telling her that it's broken."

Riesling took a step back.

Her mother wouldn't let go of her hands. "I'm so glad Trey was with you last night. I just wish you had answered our calls."

"I'm sorry, Mom. I was honestly worried I was going to get an earful of Theo and what he's been up to."

Her mother palmed her cheek. "Don't be mad at me or your father, but we know that Theo cleaned you out the last time he came into your life."

Riesling's jaw dropped. She'd been very careful about her finances in the last few months without acting as if she had been living on nothing, which she had. But Theo had promised he'd pay her back.

Right.

She knew he wouldn't, but he also had told her he would stay out of her life as well as their daughter's.

So far he'd kept his promise, but that wasn't going to last long. Only, in the last six months, she couldn't come up with a way to permanently rid Theo from her life.

She snapped her mouth shut. If her parents knew how bad it had gotten, why hadn't they offered to help instead of standing on the sidelines? Of course, they had been doing nothing for over six years except pass judgment.

"I wouldn't say he wiped me out." She swallowed her lie, though she'd managed to pay her rent. She blinked. That wouldn't be the case come the first of the month and she didn't want Trey to think she was taking advantage of their little roll in the hay or that she used him so she could get a little more time to make up the difference.

Maybe he'd just take it out of her pay.

Except she needed that for Christmas presents.

"I might not be rich, but I've got enough."

"Good to know." Her mother tilted her head. "But what are you going to do when Theo comes banging on your door with his hand held out, looking for cash? Because you know he's going to, especially now."

"Tell him to go fuck himself." Riesling squared her

shoulders. It felt good to let the words roll off her tongue. And when it came to money, she meant every single word. "But you know I can't kick him out of Ashling's life. I can't turn him away. I need you and everyone else in this family to understand and respect that. And please, don't speak ill of Theo around her. It's better if she figures out on her own what her father is made of. Even for all of us. I wouldn't want her resenting any of you."

"It's going to be hard to keep what's going on from her forever," her mother said. "But we'll do our best. You have my word."

Riesling let out a long sigh. When her mother made a promise, she kept it.

Trey

Trey stepped from the bathroom and glanced down the hallway. Carter and Weezer had just left one of the rooms.

The home office.

It wasn't the winery, but maybe there was some information about Doctor Allison and his office. Anything that would give Trey a clue as to who his parents were.

Quietly, he slipped into the office, keeping the door open so he could hear if anyone approached. His heart pounded against his chest like a wild beast.

The bookshelves were filled with books and pictures of the family. He lifted one that had Riesling and all the other siblings sitting in front of the river bend out behind the winery. He kept it clutched in one hand; that way if anyone came in, he could say he was admiring the family photographs.

He rifled through some papers on the top of the desk.

Nothing that had anything to do with the doctor. With a shaky hand, he pulled open the top drawer where he found some stationery similar to the doctor's, but again, nothing that would lead him to his parents.

He opted to examine the books on the shelf. One in particular caught his eye.

The History of Candlewood Falls.

He set the picture on the desk and opened the thick book to the index. Doctor Allison wasn't in there and that was disappointing. He flipped to the table of contents. It was organized by decade. That could be interesting.

He turned to the decade he was born.

The mayor of the town had been Jimmy Armstrong. Interesting that he was called Jimmy, and not James.

"What are you doing?" Riesling's voice bounced across the room and landed in his ears with a thud.

He jumped. "Jesus. You scared me."

"Good. Why are you snooping around my parents' office?"

"I wasn't snooping. I walked by and saw this picture of you and I wanted a closer look." He pointed to the image on the desk. "And then I saw this book and I wanted to see if it had anything about Doctor Allison."

"Why are we talking about that old quack?" Weezer appeared out of nowhere.

Talk about being busted.

But more importantly, why did Weezer call him a quack?

Time to put some shit on the line. He was taking a big risk by telling her mother anything, but Trey didn't think he was going to get anywhere if he didn't. He held Riesling's gaze as if to ask for permission.

She seemed to understand what he wanted to do since she shrugged.

"May I confide in you?" he asked, shifting his stare to Weezer.

"You better since you're standing in my private office and I don't take too kindly to that." Weezer stepped around her daughter and folded her arms and smirked.

"I apologize for that. I didn't mean to snoop." He held up the book. "Could I borrow this?"

"Maybe. First confide in me," Weezer said.

"A friend of mine was adopted and it turns out the adoption might not have been legal," he said.

"I see," Weezer said. "And what does that have to do with us?"

"The only clue my friend has as to where she might have come from is a letter from Doctor Allison to my friend's adoptive parents and the letterhead has the winery address on it."

"Shit," Weezer mumbled. "Can I see that letter?"

"I need to keep my friend's family name out of it. So, yes as long as you don't mind—"

Weezer held up her hand. "That's fine. Just get me the letter."

"Mom. Did you know about this?"

"No. Not really," Weezer said. "But your grandfather swore that Doctor Allison buried something at the winery. Your dad used to have to go out in the middle of the night and stop him from trying to unearth it. We thought Grandpa had simply lost his mind because he was talking gibberish at that point."

"Do you believe there could be anything to this story? Could Doctor Allison have facilitated illegal adoptions?" Suddenly the book in Trey's hand felt like a ton of bricks. He leaned against the desk and held his breath. This was the first real break he'd gotten, and even though it wasn't much, it was a start.

"Anything is possible," Weezer said.

Trey scratched the side of his face. "May I ask you a very personal question?"

Weezer laughed. "No. Doctor Allison wasn't my ob-gyn."

"Why not?" Trey asked.

"I didn't like him. I thought he was weird," Weezer said.

"Then why did we rent to him?" Riesling asked.

"Your grandfather made that decision before I took over and the lease was open-ended. I couldn't kick him off." Weezer took the history book from Trey's hand. "He wasn't around that much and he closed his shop about a year after Merlot was born. But he gave me a weird vibe." She tapped the book. "You should talk to Mayor Armstrong. He was close with Doctor Allison and rumor has it that he had an affair."

"With whom?" Riesling asked with wide eyes. "I can't imagine he'd do that to his wife."

"I don't know if the rumor is true, so I'm not going to repeat the name." Weezer arched a brow. "Talk with Mayor Armstrong and see what he says. If you get nowhere with him, I might give up the name, but if I do that, I want to know for whom I'm doing it for. Got it?"

Trey nodded. "That's fair."

"Now get out of my office." Weezer pointed.

Trey tucked the book under his arm and made a beeline for the hallway, right behind Riesling. He followed her straight to the back deck where she turned on her heel and poked him in the chest.

"What the hell was that?" she asked. "Why on earth would you think it's okay to go snooping around my parents' house?"

"That's not what I was doing."

"Right. I don't believe you," she said with venom dripping from her words. "Who is this woman that you're doing all this digging for and what does she mean to you?"

"She's just a family friend."

"Nope. I don't buy that shit." Riesling tucked her hair behind her ears.

He worried she might tear the cartilage right off her head.

"It's true."

"There's more to the story than that and I'd appreciate the truth."

And he owed her that. But this wasn't the time or the place. "Can we talk about this when we're not surrounded by your entire family?"

"You're off the hook for a few days but—"

"A few days?" he questioned.

"Eliza Jane and I are going into the city to go shopping for her wedding dress and Malbec surprised us today with a two-night stay at a spa."

"That was nice of him."

"Agreed, but when I get back, you and I are going to have a conversation and I want names and explanations."

He nodded. Perhaps it was time to be honest.

About everything.

Carter

Carter paced in his home office in front of his massive desk. Well, it wasn't his anymore; it was his wife's— who was actually his ex-wife—but he'd soon remedy that. Of course, Weezer wanted to live together first. Another trial run.

Well, he'd give that woman whatever she wanted.

"Hey, honey. Looks like we both needed to have a discussion with each other." Weezer gently closed the door and strolled across the room. She wrapped her loving arms around him and kissed his lips.

He savored the moment as long as he could before he took a step back and leaned against the desk, gripping the sides. Sometimes her kisses made him feel like a damned teenaged boy. He cleared his throat. "Can I go first?"

"Of course," she said.

"I have some bad news and I wanted you to hear it from me before it's all over town."

"That sounds serious. Should I be sitting down?"

Carter nodded.

Weezer took a seat in the corner wingback chair. She crossed her legs and set her hands in her lap. She could be a patient woman where Carter was concerned.

Not so much anyone else.

"Harry texted me. Theo landed at Newark airport

about an hour ago. He asked his father if he could come home."

"I hope Harry told him where he could go."

Carter laughed. "I can tell you Harry told him not to come to Candlewood Falls, but we both know Theo isn't going to listen. I suspect he won't stay in town. Maybe a hotel close by, but I'm sure we'll be seeing him soon enough."

"I tried to get Riesling to admit she was broke, but she wouldn't."

"Please tell me you didn't offer her money. The last thing we need is for her to go running off again." Carter ran a hand across the top of his head. "She's just like you when it comes to keeping her word and she told us if we ever pulled a stunt like we did three years ago, we might not ever see her or Ashling again."

"Honestly, Carter. I believe we're past that with her, but I agree. We can't take the risk. She and I are getting along so well. I don't want to mess that up and I love having her live so close. I never want to lose that again."

"Are you turning soft on me?"

"They say age does that to a woman." She hugged herself. "Especially around the middle."

Carter shook his head. He wasn't touching that one with a ten-foot pole.

"By the way, I need to borrow the pickup sometime next week."

"Why?"

"I'm going to be dumping some of the things that Trey is throwing away and I finally cleared out two of the upstairs rooms."

"I can take them to the dump for you."

"No. I'm going to be putting them in different dumpsters through town."

"Excuse me?" Carter had seen his wife do some strange things over the years, but this was about as bizarre as it got. "Why the hell would you do that?"

"I saw Lyra Chambers dumpster diving. When I did a little more research, I found out she does that on a regular basis. Some of this stuff is in really good shape, so if we can help her furnish that place, so be it. We know that snobby mother of hers isn't going to do anything but make her feel like a failure."

"Sometimes I wonder if that's what we've done with Riesling." Carter let out a long breath. "I stand by giving her that ultimatum when she left with Theo, but I don't want her to feel like she can't come to us."

"I'm trying, Carter. I really am. I all but offered her money and we both know if I had, she'd take that as an insult. She's a proud woman and she's an amazing mother. I only want what's best for her."

Carter smiled. "It's going to work out. I'm going to find Theo and I'm going to make sure he stays out of our lives."

"I'm going to trust you on this one."

"Good. Now, what is it that you wanted to talk to me about?"

"The secrets that are buried on this fucking winery."

Carter arched a brow. "And what secrets are we talking about now because I thought we covered the one that nearly destroyed our family."

"This is the one that my father believed Doctor Allison buried by the overflow building."

"Jesus. That again? Why are we talking about that now?"

"Because Trey is digging it up," she said. "He's looking into an illegal adoption that leads back to him and a letter with our winery address. I told him to go talk with Mayor Armstrong."

"He was rumored to be having an affair with Janet Sprouse."

"I know, but I didn't tell Trey that. Only that Armstrong might know something."

"But he's not going to tell Trey anything," Carter said.

"Probably not, but I never trusted Allison. I always thought he was up to something. So, I want to find out what the hell was going on before Trey does and that's the other thing. I doubt Trey's looking for a friend. I bet he's the illegal adoption without answers which now pisses me off because I know he spent the night with Riesling last night and if he's playing her, he'll have to answer to me."

Carter closed the gap and took Weezer by the hands, helping her to her feet. "He'll be answering to the both of us, but put yourself in his shoes. Would you be honest about what you were looking for?"

"Well, no."

"Then cut him some slack. He's a good man trying to figure out where he came from. Let's try to help him instead of judge him." He pressed his finger against Weezer's lips. "Let's worry about Theo first. Then we'll deal with this Allison thing."

10

RIESLING

"**I** slept with him." Riesling took a step back and stared at her future sister-in-law in the mirror. She looked stunning in the simple floor-length wedding dress with long sleeves and a lace overlay. It didn't have a ton of detail. Just enough.

And it was this soft candle-white color that complemented her complexion. They had tried on five dresses, but this one by far outshined the rest of them.

"I'm not surprised." Eliza Jane twisted and turned with a beaming smile. "It's obvious the two of you have chemistry."

"That doesn't mean I had to invite him to my bed, and it was right after I found out that Theo was being investigated."

Eliza Jane stepped off the pedestal and lifted her glass of champagne. "I'm not supposed to tell you this, but you're going to find out anyway." She took a small dainty sip of her beverage. "Theo's in New Jersey."

Riesling groaned. "How is it that you know this and I don't?" Panic filled her gut. They were supposed to stay in the city for another night, but how could she when Theo could be waltzing into her daughter's life any second.

"Malbec is freaking out over it. He saw Theo this morning when he was driving to the winery. He went straight to your dad who confirmed he knew through Harry that Theo had landed on Thanksgiving." Eliza Jane waved her finger. "I don't pretend to understand all the dynamics of this family or this town yet. But Ashling is with Weezer over at the alpaca farm with Brooklyn and Caleb."

"Good. Theo won't go anywhere near Caleb, or Brooklyn for that matter. He's terrified of Brooklyn's dad and once he finds out Caleb is back in town, he'll stay as far away from him as possible. But that's not going to stop him from seeing her. Not if my folks take her into town or if he shows up at their place, which he has the balls to do."

"Which is why we're going home right after I buy this dress."

"I can't do that to you. This is supposed to be your weekend."

She waved her hand. "We can take a spa day anytime we want. Protecting Ashling is a lot more important."

"That dress is perfect." Riesling smiled. She needed to get her mind off Theo. There was nothing she could do right now and obsessing over it wasn't going to help.

"I know, right." Eliza Jane did a little twirl. "It will just take me a minute to change." She ducked behind the curtain. "Now tell me all about Trey. He seems like a really nice guy."

"I caught him snooping in my mom's home office." Riesling slumped in the chair in the corner of the massive dressing room.

"What?" Eliza Jane poked her head between the two pieces of fabric. "What on earth was he doing?"

"He said he noticed the pictures and then a history book, but he's on this mission to find out about an illegal adoption that Doctor Allison might have facilitated."

"Malbec has talked about him," Eliza Jane said. "And the possibility he might have buried something on the winery."

"That's possible, but what really gets me is that Trey is doing all this for another woman."

"Oh." Eliza Jane emerged from the small dressing room carrying her wedding dress and a glow.

Riesling's heart swelled. Knowing that her brother finally found a true partner made her soul happy.

"Do you know who she is to Trey? Has she come to visit him or anything?"

"Not that I know of," Riesling said. "He says her

parents are family friends and he's doing it more for them, but the fact he'd go sneaking around my mother's house tells me this means a lot more to him than doing a friend a favor."

"I agree," Eliza Jane said. "Have you talked to him about it?"

"No, but after Mom and I caught him—"

"Weezer found him in her office?" Eliza Jane paused with her fingers curled around the doorknob. She stared at Riesling with wild eyes. "What did she do?"

"Not what you'd expect, exactly."

"She's changed in the last couple of months." Eliza Jane stepped into the main area of the dress shop.

"That's all because she's not carrying around that lie anymore," Riesling said. "Anyway. I told Trey that when I get back, I want answers. I want the woman's name. What she means to him and why this is so damn important."

"What did he say?"

"He agreed and he better be honest or I'm out of a job and I'm actually going to have to do what I swore I would never do."

Eliza Jane handed the salesclerk her off-the-rack dress and glared at Riesling. "You'd seriously move back in with one of your parents?"

"I'm seriously broke."

"When our house is done, you can come live with us." Eliza Jane looped her arm around Riesling.

"My brother might have something to say about that."

"Yeah. He'll say, *yes, dear. Whatever you say, dear.*"

"You two really do make the cutest couple ever and I've never seen my brother so happy." Riesling laughed. It was more a nervous laugh than a funny one because if Trey lied to her about any of this, or if he was even sort of involved with another woman, not only would she be devastated, but it would prove to her that she couldn't pick a man for shit.

Eliza Jane handed her credit card to the salesperson. Riesling had never been married and Theo hadn't ever asked. He told her when they packed up her things and left Candlewood Falls that as soon as they got settled, he'd buy her a ring and they could start their life.

She knew before they drove out of town that she was making a mistake, but she didn't know what else to do. Malbec and her mother were barely speaking. Chablis and Merlot had their issues with the family while the three youngest River children didn't understand everything that was going on, yet. Only, all six of them had wanted to be a part of The River Winery future. It left Riesling in the odd position as the only one who had no desire to work for the family business in any capacity.

It had been another bone of contention with her mother.

"It's crazy how quickly this has happened." Eliza Jane signed the slip. "Never in a million years did I think I'd be getting married anytime soon. And I can't believe I found the perfect dress and on sale to boot." She held up the receipt. "Off the rack is the only way to go."

"If I were to ever get married, I'd want to wear my mom's dress." That had been the real kicker when she'd left with Theo. Her mother had told her that she could kiss that dress goodbye.

"I've seen it and it's absolutely beautiful. It would look stunning on you."

"Thanks, but I doubt I'll ever be getting married. Most guys don't want a built-in family." Nor did they want the bullshit that came with her daughter's father.

"That brings us full circle right back to Trey." Eliza Jane folded her dress that had been wrapped nice and neat in a wedding bag over her arm. "I can tell you really like him."

"More than I should," Riesling admitted.

"I've never understood what that meant."

Riesling lifted her cell and found the ride sharing app. Their hotel was about ten blocks away. They could get a train back to New Jersey in two hours and she'd be home in time to tuck her daughter in for the night.

"I don't know Trey outside of the fact I believe he's an excellent doctor. He's really great with his patients and I like working for him, but he hasn't revealed much about who he is except he'll go snooping around to find out information that might involve my family for another woman."

"You're jealous," Eliza Jane said matter-of-factly.

"I am not."

Eliza Jane wrapped her free arm around Riesling. "It's a normal reaction under the circumstances. Just ask him when we get back and then go on a real date. That's what you need. Malbec and I will take Ashling for the night. It will be good practice for us."

Riesling snapped her gaze to her future sister-in-law. "Practice?"

Eliza Jane nodded. "You're the first to know. Well, except for your brother and he's a hot mess."

"That's amazing. My parents are going to go apeshit."

"That's kind of why we haven't said anything yet. We might wait until after the wedding, or maybe at the wedding, so I need you to keep the secret."

"I can do that." Her cell vibrated in her hand. "Our ride is here."

"Oh my goodness. I don't know why I didn't think of it before now," Eliza Jane said. "I talked your brother into doing that Victorian Christmas Tour. You and Trey should go."

Riesling groaned.

"We could double date and Trey might like learning all about the houses around town. What do you say?"

"I guess so." As long as Trey was truthful, a date seemed like the appropriate next step.

Trey

Trey stood in front of the printer and waited for the documents to finish dropping into the tray. Everything his father had on his adoption, with all the names, nothing blacked out. He glanced at his watch. Riesling had gotten home late last night, something about Theo being in town.

Fucking jerk.

If Trey ran into that asshole, he wasn't sure he'd be able to keep his mouth closed.

He took the papers and meandered into the residence kitchen, which was on the second floor. It was a nice temporary setup and he knew he'd be in Candlewood Falls until he found answers, and then he'd put the practice up for sale, citing he wasn't cut out for small-town doctoring.

Only, the entire concept had grown on him and it wasn't just the fact he couldn't get Riesling out of his mind. She was one of the first things he thought about when he woke in the morning and he certainly enjoyed drifting off to sleeping dreaming about her.

Staring out the window, he could see her strolling down the dirt road, which had a dusting of snow. He couldn't believe it was almost the first of December and soon Christmas would be rolling around. It was his mother's favorite holiday. She loved it so much, and the day after Thanksgiving, she'd start in on the decorations, which were extensive. Not a room in the house went untouched with winter wonderland. It took his mom a good week to finish and as much as she complained about how little he and his father helped, when they tried all she did was bitch that they did it all wrong.

The doorbell rang. He'd installed one of those cameras with an app where he could see and talk to whoever was standing at the threshold.

"Door's open. Come on up," he said.

Quickly, he refilled his coffee mug and headed into the family room.

Time to face the music.

The way he saw it, this could go only one of two ways. She was either going to be very understanding or she was going to hate him for the rest of his life and he'd have to respect her wishes.

He sat in his favorite egg-shaped chair and set the papers facedown on the table. He still wouldn't be able to tell her who his father's friend was, but he would be honest about how he switched things around.

If his mother were alive, she'd be explaining to him how it's better to be honest before jumping into bed with someone. He absolutely didn't regret sleeping with Riesling, though maybe he should because even if she found it in her heart to accept his reasons for lying to her, he had no idea if he could commit to this kind of life.

"Good morning." She appeared at the top of the stairs.

"I'm sorry you had to cut your trip short. Have you seen your ex?"

She shook her head. "And neither has Ashling, which is a good thing. But it's only a matter of time."

"Have you talked to his parents? Have they seen him?" Shit. He sounded like a nosy asshole. Just because he'd slept with her once didn't give him the right to be this interested in her personal life, especially in regard to her daughter. A mother-child relationship was a delicate dance. Even more so when the father was in and out of Ashling's life and that was compounded by Theo's recent alleged criminal activity.

"I've spoken to Harry," Riesling said. "And he's told his son that he's not welcome in this town, or in their lives. That ship has sailed, but to his knowledge, Theo has not left New Jersey."

"What are you going to do?" Trey honestly wanted to support and help her when it came to her ex; however, he knew he was in part avoiding the reason for this meeting.

She kicked off her shoes and sat on the sofa, tucking her feet up under her butt. She took a piece of her hair and twisted it between her fingers.

She looked relaxed and contemplative at the same time. "He's her father. He has a visitation rights. I can't deny him," she said with thick emotion. "I'm tired of explaining this to everyone, including you." She tilted her head. "I don't want to waste time with small talk. Who is this woman that you're willing to go poking around my mom's home office for?"

He shifted, uncrossing his legs and recrossing them. His heart pounded like a woodpecker going to town on his favorite tree. "There are two things I need to tell you."

"I'm listening." She continued to twist her hair between her forefinger and thumb.

He couldn't tell if that was a nervous thing, if she was bored, or if it was something else entirely. Whatever it was, it made him slightly uncomfortable.

"There is no woman friend. Not really." He held up his hand. He couldn't have her interrupt and ask a million questions. He'd never get through it all in the way that would make the most sense. "My father knows this high-profile man who got his mistress pregnant back in the day. He used Doctor Allison to give the baby up for adoption."

"So, you're trying to find out where this baby went?"

There was no stopping Riesling from her questions.

"No," Trey said. "This woman who gave up a kid, it was a girl, so I reversed the situation and pretended she was the person I was looking for when in reality this is the person who wants to find their birth parents." Hoping his fingers didn't twitch or his hands didn't shake, he lifted all the documents he'd gathered, leaned over, and handed her the papers. He could have just said his name. That would have been the less cowardly thing to do and certainly less dramatic.

However, he couldn't bring his vocal cords to say the words.

She held his gaze for a long moment before glancing at the white sheets with black type. "What is this?"

"Just read the top one. The one with the winery stationery. It will make sense in the first paragraph."

"Dear Mr. Jefferson, I have found what you are looking for. If you are still interested, please sign the enclosed contract and send a check for ten thousand dollars. The adoption will be sealed and closed. The mother is due in three weeks. I will induce a week early. Please remember this is private and confidential. I look forward to hearing from you."

Riesling dropped her hands to her lap. "You were adopted? You're the one looking for your birth parents? Why the fuck didn't you just tell me that?"

"Because I thought it would be easier if I found out where my father's friend's baby went, but I can't find his records either."

"And who is he?"

"You have to promise me you won't tell anyone and I'm also hoping you won't tell your family about what I'm doing."

She furrowed her brow. "I can't make that promise if it's going to hurt them or my family's business. But I will keep it to myself for now."

If Trey wanted her help, and her trust, he was going

to have to live with that answer. Besides, he owed her the truth.

He took in a deep breath. This shouldn't be so difficult but he found himself feeling as though he could be losing a friend and that hurt his heart in ways he couldn't understand. Riesling had come to mean more to him than anyone he'd met in a long time. He wanted her in his life and he didn't know how to deal with that emotion or where to store it in his brain. "Greg Levine is a good friend of my dad's."

"The television personality? He was born in Candlewood Falls."

That little piece of information Trey hadn't known, and that pissed him off. Greg should have told him that.

"How long did he live here?"

"Not long," Riesling said. "But it's in that history book you borrowed from my mother's place."

"I didn't see that in there. I haven't read that much. I've been organizing all the files that I can find that have Doctor Allison's name on it." Trey lifted his coffee mug, wishing he'd made it of the Irish variety. "I was trying to see if maybe Levine's ex-girlfriend, the woman he had the affair with, was in the files, but she's not."

"So, you know her?"

Trey nodded. "She was a model back then and the pregnancy ruined her career. Not because people found out, but because she had to take the time off. She ended up going on to be a pretty well-known actress who doesn't want anyone to know about her affair with Levine or that she gave up a child. I've interviewed both of them. They told me the process on their end and my father told me what they had to do in order to get a baby. But what I can't find are the records to match me to my birth parents."

Riesling set the rest of the papers on the coffee table. She'd stopped twirling her hair and tucked it behind her ears. "Why is it so important for you to find out who they are? It's obvious you adore the people who adopted you and you see them as your family."

He ran a hand over his face. "The people who raised me are my mom and dad. I don't question that. And even though I'm angry that they lied to me, they will always be my family. But I want to know where I came from and why they either didn't want me or couldn't keep me." He tapped his chest. "It's like there is this constant fire in my heart burning a hole and it won't stop until I have answers."

"Have you always known you were adopted?"

"Yes. But not the point. After my mother died, she left me a note and that letter."

"That's kind of shitty."

He nodded. "I just want to know the biology and the why." He blew out a puff of air and glanced toward the ceiling. "And since there are two babies that I know about, I feel like there has to be more."

"Curiosity often kills the cat, but now I'm intrigued and my mom mentioned Armstrong having an affair and that makes me think he used Doctor Allison and maybe my mom knows or suspects more than she's letting on."

"Do you really believe that? Would your mom keep such a dark secret?"

Riesling laughed. "If she doesn't know it to be true for sure. If it's all rumor and she doesn't have proof, she won't dare repeat it. However, if she knows something for sure, forget about it, she'll spread it all over town, unless she has a good reason not to."

"I don't know why that reminds me of *Dexter* and the idea that he only kills bad people," Trey said.

"That's actually a good way to describe my mom."

"I figured I'd call Jimmy Armstrong tomorrow, but I don't know what my angle would be to get him to agree to a sit-down."

"You don't need one," Riesling said. "My father is meeting him Thursday in town for a light dinner to discuss some legal matter. You and I will make sure we run into them and you can at the very least set something up. It will be less awkward."

"That sounds like a good plan. Thank you." He was slightly surprised that she was agreeable to helping him, especially after he lied.

"Also, Armstrong's house is on the Victorian Christmas Tour. I thought you and I could go. He and his wife always greet people and I could maybe distract them and you could snoop. Though you might want to hone your skills a bit."

"Ouch," he said, but he deserved the jab. "I'm sorry I wasn't honest with you about all of this. I don't want to open a can of worms and hurt a bunch of people, but can you understand where I'm coming from?"

"I can. It's part of why I will never speak badly of Ashling's father in front of her. That's where she came from. I can't change the biology and if I'm the one filling her impressionable mind on the kind of person he is, then she'll resent me."

"But you have to protect her from—"

"Don't you dare," she said with a harsh tone. "I know exactly the kind of man Theo is and Ashling is never alone with him. That's all part of the custody and visitation. So, when he does show up, his visits have to be with myself or someone in my family present. Theo knows better than to push me on that because it could land him in front of a judge, something he doesn't want considering he's constantly getting himself in some kind of trouble. The older Ashling gets, the more she'll see what kind of person her dad is and maybe she'll be mad at me for a minute and a half when he breaks her heart, but at least she won't resent me for tainting her opinion."

"That's not what I was going to say." Trey understood where Riesling was coming from, and he agreed. Completely. "She might be only six, but the local news keeps playing the story over and over again. It's on the front page of the paper. She's going to hear about what Theo is tangled up in and this is one of those things that might be best if she hears it from her mother so you can explain things in a way a child can relate before she sees her father." This was literally none of his business. He shouldn't be saying anything at all, only he cared a great deal for both mother and daughter. When he left Candlewood Falls, he would miss them. He could feel that deep in his bones and he knew it was a sensation he'd never shake. "I'm not suggesting you tell her he's an asshole and a criminal, but who knows what message she might get if it's filtered through someone else's eyes."

Riesling dropped her head back. "This is so fucking unfair. I don't need this crap in my life, but you're right and I plan on taking Ashling to a special lunch today."

"Would you like some company?"

"No. I need to do this myself, but I appreciate the offer."

"Well, I'm here for any kind of moral support you might need."

She glanced at her watch. "I need to pick her up in two hours. Until then, why don't we go looking through all the files you have sorted and thumb through that history book. I'll make a list of things for you to look for in the library, and this week, we can start playing Nancy Drew and the Hardy Boys."

"I was hoping to be Sherlock Holmes, but one of the Hardy boys will work." He stood, stretching out his arm.

Thankfully, she took his hand.

He pulled her close to his chest. He wanted to wrap his arms around her body, but decided it was best to clarify where he stood.

"Are we good?" he asked. "Because it's important to me that not only our working relationship remain intact, but that our personal one does too."

"Professional, we're hunky-dory," she said. "Personally, that all depends on if you ever lie to me again."

"I don't plan on it."

"Better not." She patted his pectoral. "Let's go organize some files and find some clues."

At least he knew he wasn't in the doghouse, which was an odd feeling because being in a relationship with Riesling shouldn't be on his agenda.

But it was and he couldn't talk himself out of it if he tried.

11

TREY

T rey ran his finger over a picture of Jimmy Armstrong, the former mayor of Candlewood Falls.

There was something so familiar about him, especially in the eyes. They were dark, like milk chocolate and reminded him of his own.

But so did a lot of people who had dark eyes. For the last few years, he'd been looking at older men and women for any kind of recognition. Any kind of spark that someone might be his father or mother. But that was like looking for a needle in a haystack.

A pipe dream.

There was a part of Trey that wondered if he'd left his practice in the city and moved to Candlewood Falls not so much because he was desperate to find out where he'd come from, but more because he needed a break from who he'd become after his divorce and after his mother's death.

However, he had to admit, something about Armstrong felt familiar.

He pulled another book down from the library shelf and carried it to the table. The history of Candlewood Falls was fascinating all by itself.

"Hey there," a woman's voice said.

Trey glanced up and smiled. "Zinfandel. How are you?"

Riesling's sister plopped herself in the chair across the table. "I'm awesome. What's going on with you?"

"Are you always this full of pep?"

"Pretty much," she said. "What are you doing here?"

"I've found myself a little fascinated by the history of your little town and these two." He pushed the book about Mayor Armstrong across the table and then the newspaper clipping about Doctor Allison and his delivery of twins on the side of the road.

"Jimmy and his wife have been around forever," Zinfandel said. "He's a sweet old man. My sister, Chablis, dated his son, Junior, for a bit. It was a match basically made in hell, but Junior isn't the worst guy."

"You're going to think I'm a total gossip, and I'm not. I'm just sitting here reading all these books and since I'm not from a small town, my mind is wandering like a crazy man. Do you think Armstrong has been faithful to his wife this entire time?"

Zinfandel leaned back and smiled. She had the same grin as her mom and as Riesling. It was bright and full of sass. It was something completely magical and if he could bottle it and sell it as a potion, he'd make a lot of money. "There has been a rumor or two that Armstrong had a mistress back in the day. But I've never heard a name. It's like it's the best-kept secret in this town." She leaned forward, folding her arms across the table. "Why are you so curious about an old man's past sex life?"

Trey chuckled.

"Or is it something else you're after? Like secrets buried on my family's winery?"

He tilted his head. "What makes you think that?"

She shrugged. "I'm observant and I overhear things. I'm also curious and being the youngest, I missed out on all the good gossip. Now I stick my nose in it wherever possible. Though, much like everyone else in my family, I'm careful not to repeat shit that isn't true."

"So, what can you tell me about this that's factual?"

"That's an interesting question." Zinfandel let out a long breath. "Sadly, I don't have much that I can tell you. It's all rumors and if I were to repeat any of it, I'm afraid you might end up with biased opinions or have the wrong idea about people."

"I find it fascinating that your entire family all feels the same way."

"We know people who have been hurt by lies that have been spread, including my mom. So it's pretty much the code we've learned to live by," Zinfandel said. "However, if you tell me what it is you're after, I can try to shed some light on it."

This was his chance to get a little bit of information. Even if it was hearsay or gossip or half-truths. It was better than nothing. He needed a lead. Anything. He didn't care. Something that would give him a path to chase.

"I think Doctor Allison was running an illegal adoption program of some kind."

Zinfandel's eyebrows shot up. "Seriously? Have you mentioned this to my sister?"

He nodded. No point in lying. "I'm not sure she'd appreciate me saying something to you, for the same reasons you mentioned a few moments ago."

"I won't promise to keep this conversation to myself," Zinfandel said. "If Riesling asks me what I did today or if for some reason it comes up, I'll tell her I ran into you and what we talked about."

"She knows I think Allison might have been doing something weird."

"What does Riesling believe?"

If he were to answer that honestly, he'd have to tell Zinfandel his story and he wasn't ready to do that yet. "That I don't have much to go on."

"Well, my grandfather believed that Doctor Allison buried something on our winery and that whatever it was, it wasn't good. He was so crazy about it near the end of his life that he would go digging around for it. I don't remember that, but I do recall everyone talking about it when I got older. I did once overhear my grandfather yelling at my mom that she didn't understand. That if he didn't find it, it would someday come back and haunt some of the good people of Candlewood Falls. That what he'd done might have been considered a good thing and by all rights it was, but it was also a bad thing."

That didn't tell him one damn thing. "That's kind of cryptic, but doesn't really help me any."

"But it does," Zinfandel said. "Because whatever was buried out there has never been found. You find that, and you've got your answers." Zinfandel flattened her hands against the table and stood. "I better get going. See you later."

Well, that was interesting.

And truthful.

Maybe he needed to go digging.

Riesling

Riesling stood at the top of stairs with her cell glued to her ear. "Why are you telling me this?"

"You don't find it weird that Trey was in the library digging up information on Armstrong and Allison?"

"What I find utterly fascinating is that you're turning into a gossip."

"No. That's actually the furthest thing from the truth." Zinfandel sighed. "It's not the first time I've heard that about Allison."

"What are you talking about? What have you heard and how reliable is it?"

"I have a friend that I went to college with who was adopted as well as her two older siblings. The oldest sister who is thirty-nine went looking for her birth parents years ago and kept hitting dead ends where all her siblings found their biological families. The more she pushed, the more she found discrepancies and those oddities landed her right here in Candlewood Falls and Doctor Allison. I haven't said anything to my friend because what is there to say except rumor and gossip about shit I don't know anything about. But seriously, do you think Doctor Allison could have buried information about illegal adoptions on our property?"

"I'd say it's a pretty good possibility." Riesling didn't see the point in lying to her family. "I think it's something we should consider looking into, but let me handle it, okay?"

"You can take lead, but my friend would like answers."

"I'll keep you in the loop."

"Thanks," Zinfandel said before hanging up.

Riesling stuffed her cell in her back pocket and turned her attention toward her daughter's bedroom.

Ashling sat in her bed and fiddled with her stuffed animal and a book.

"Are you all ready for bed?" Riesling asked.

"Yes, Mommy." Ashling lifted her gaze and smiled. "Can I ask you a question?"

"Of course, baby girl." Riesling sat on the edge of her daughter's bed. "What do you want to know?"

"Do you like Trey?"

"Of course I do."

"No. I mean like a boyfriend."

"Why are you asking me that?" Riesling took the book and set it on the nightstand.

"Because if I were a grown-up, I'd want him to be my boyfriend."

"Oh. I see." Riesling pulled the covers up over her daughter. "For now, he's just a really good friend."

"Does that mean his status could change?"

Status? God. Her daughter was amazing smart. "It could," she said. "Do you have any other questions for Mommy?"

Ashling's eyelids fluttered over her precious baby blues. "Are the police going to arrest Daddy?"

"I don't know, sweat pea. Your father is being accused of something; that doesn't mean he did it."

"But you think he did." Ashling stretched her arms up over her head before rolling to her side. "I bet Grandma and Grandpa River believe he did it."

"It doesn't matter what we believe or not. The truth is what is important and that might take some time for everyone to figure out."

Ashling tucked her little hands under her cheek. "If Daddy said he didn't do it, would the police leave him alone?"

Out of the mouths of babes.

"It doesn't work that way," Riesling explained. "There are other people who have said Daddy took their money and didn't do what he said he was going to do with it. It's one person's word against the others."

"That means someone is lying."

Shit. Her kid was way too smart for her own good.

"I don't want you to worry about any of this." She ran her hand across her little girl's head. "But I needed to tell you what was going on because people are going to be talking about it and your father is going to be in town."

Ashling blinked. "Is he staying with Grandma and Grandpa Richardson?"

"That's not likely." How did she tell her baby girl that she hadn't heard a single word from Theo and had no idea if he would even bother? Or worse, that she hoped he'd stay flying under the radar for as long as he stayed anywhere in the state of New Jersey. If she never saw Theo again, it would be too soon.

She leaned over and kissed Ashling's forehead. "I haven't spoken to your dad, so I don't know what his plans are and I'm not sure your grandparents do either."

"Daddy makes Grandma Richardson cry and I heard Grandpa say the last time I was there that he's had it and won't put up with it anymore. That he's going to tell Daddy not to come around anymore. Do you think Grandpa Richardson has done that and maybe Daddy already left town?"

"How would you feel if that were true?" It was more important to address the idea that Theo had come and gone and didn't have the time to see his daughter. Now that was a reality Riesling could deal with.

Ashling yawned. "I only miss him after I see him, not before."

What an interesting way to put it and it made perfect sense in the eyes of a small child.

"If you see your dad, I need you to tell me, okay? And if he shows up at school or somewhere I'm not, you can't go with him. I'm sorry. I know it's hard for you to understand why, but that's just how it has to be."

Ashling lifted her hand and palmed Riesling's cheek. "I know, Mommy. I understand. I won't go anywhere with Daddy, and I promise to find you or one of my grandparents if Daddy tries to contact me. Or maybe Trey. Would that be okay?"

A warmth spread across Riesling's skin. It was as if she'd stepped onto a tropical beach in the middle of the afternoon and there wasn't a single cloud in the sky.

She'd tried to stay mad at Trey for lying to her but that had been an impossible concept in part because she knew she probably would have done the exact same thing if she were in his shoes.

"Yes. If Trey is the only grown-up around, he would be fine." Riesling kissed her daughter's cheek. "Now, get some sleep, baby girl." She turned the lamp off and tiptoed out of the bedroom. She stood in the doorway for a long moment and stared at her sweet little girl. It took only a minute before Ashling was sound asleep.

Riesling couldn't believe how well her kid handled the entire situation, but she worried that there would be an emotional scar that somehow affected Ashling in a negative way for the rest of her life. That thought had been haunting Riesling for as long as she could remember. The last thing she wanted to do was leave the kind of legacy that would be a burden to her kid. She wanted something better for her baby. That's one of the reasons she never wanted a job on the winery. Not that she didn't believe in the family business, because she did, but when she did have a family of her own, she didn't want her kids to have that kind of obligation, so she had to break free for them.

Although, Riesling had no talent for winemaking and her passion had always been helping others. Her father understood that even when her mother hadn't.

She sighed. Her mom hadn't been upset or disappointed that Riesling went into the medical field. No.

She'd all but disowned Riesling because she had chosen Theo over family.

As Riesling made her way downstairs for a glass of wine, she allowed herself to feel what it would be like if a grown-up Ashling had met someone like Theo and she made the same choice. A sharp pain tore right in the center of Riesling's heart. There was no way in hell she'd ever admit to her mom that she'd been right because the way in which her mom had cut her out had been so brutal, it could have destroyed all ties. What had held them together these last six years had been always been Ashling's unconditional love, even before she had the ability to speak and express it.

That and the fact that Riesling never wanted to lose her family. Deep down she'd known picking Theo had been an act of defiance and eventually she was going to have to come home with her tail between her legs. Only, she was going to do it with as much pride as she could and that meant doing it on her terms, not her parents'.

A dark shadow grew taller in the trees that lined the backyard. She held her breath as she stared at it while she patted the counter for her phone. She could have sworn she left it there when she'd gone upstairs to tuck in her little girl. Keeping her eyes focused on the figure slinking under the moonlight, she found her cell. "Hey Siri, call Trey," she whispered.

She rationalized that he was the closest person and could get to her the fastest.

"Riesling? Is everything okay?"

"No. I think someone is watching me," she said with a shaky voice, which she resented. The only person who would be lurking in the shadows of the night would be her fucking ex. Damn asshole didn't have the nerve to show his face because he knew the well was dried up. She had nothing left to give and this time using their daughter wasn't going to do him any good. All it was going to do was break Ashling's heart and Riesling needed to make sure that didn't happen.

But how?

"I'm on my way over. Stay on the line with me."

"I need to call my father." She let out a long breath. Asking her dad for legal help was breaking a pact she'd made with herself six years ago. But standing frozen in her kitchen, she realized she'd surrounded herself with family because she needed them.

When Malbec had returned, he told Riesling that being an island hadn't done anything to resolve his issues with their mother. All it had done was create a bigger body of water to swim back home through.

And he was right. The longer she stayed away, keeping her problems locked up in her heart, the harder it all became and the lonelier she became. The worst part was it solved absolutely nothing except it kept a wedge between her and her mother.

She was so tired of fighting with her mom. She wanted life to go back to when she could tell her mother anything and even if her mom teased her a little bit, it was better than the raging river that flowed between them now.

"That call can wait until I know you're safe." Trey's voice sounded winded. "Can you see anyone?"

"No. And the shadow is gone." She leaned closer to the windowpane.

Nothing.

Whoever was out there either slinked back into the safety of the brush or had left. Or was never there in the first place.

All equally disturbing.

"I'm at the front door. Let me in," Trey said.

She raced through her house, nearly tripping over the welcome rug. Tossing the cell on the sofa to the right, she tugged open the door and tossed herself into Trey's arms. "If there was someone out there, it was Theo out there. I can't imagine anyone else lurking around in the bushes." She clung to Trey as if he were the roots of her tree. The foundation for home.

Her rock.

Her body trembled in his embrace and he held tight.

She found the kind of comfort in his embrace that she'd been searching for her entire life. It was warm, kind, and gentle.

Caring.

"I came through the woods and I didn't see anyone, but that doesn't mean someone wasn't there," he whispered in her ear before pressing his tender lips against her temple. "I heard a car take off at the road just as I entered by the dirt road, but I couldn't see the car." Trey cupped her cheeks. "Do you want to call the police?"

She shook her head. It wouldn't be the first time she thought she saw something and it was nothing. Besides, Theo was a lot of things, but violent wasn't one of them. "It's not going to do any good. It's not like there's a warrant out for his arrest or anything."

"The authorities do want to talk with him and he's not making that easy for them." Trey kissed her forehead. Her cheek. Her neck, just below her ear.

A warm tingle floated across her skin, starting at her head and landing on her toes. She stared into his dark-chocolate eyes and swallowed. "I don't want to get tangled up in whatever he's done. I only want him out of mine and Ashling's life for good and in order to do that, I need my father's help."

"It's late. Why don't we call him first thing in the morning."

Trey was right. There was no point in enlisting her dad's help right this second. He could begin drawing up whatever legal documents she needed in the morning. Her father had hinted a few times that if and when she was ready to have Theo permanently removed from their lives, he'd be ready, but that she'd have to be willing to go the distance.

"Do you really believe Ashling will be okay if I make it so her father can't ever see her again until she's an adult?"

Trey cupped her face. "I generally don't make this kind of judgment. However, based on the things you've told me, and your family, yes. She's better off without the yo-yo ride, especially if what the news is reporting is true."

"Deep down, I know it's true. He's stolen from people in the past. Theo isn't a good person."

"Why are you so hell-bent on keeping Theo in Ashling's life?"

"I'm not." She curled her fingers around his wrists and took a step back. She'd never quite been able to explain all this proper. It always came out that she didn't want to be hated and judged by her daughter, much like she resented her own mother.

But there was so much more to the story than her own broken relationships.

For her entire life, up until she left Candlewood Falls, her decisions had been made for her. Even when she'd decided she didn't want to go into the family business, her mother had a hand in where she went to school and how she became a physician's assistant, right down to where she worked, and the worst part was that Riesling let her do it all under the pretense that she'd actually had control over her own life.

Riesling even believed she'd taken charge when she made the horrible choice to run off with Theo.

However, all she'd done was transfer power from her mother to Theo.

Instead of taking it all for herself.

All she wanted was for her daughter to have the confidence in herself to trust her own decision-making abilities. The only way to do that was not to push her own ideals, opinions, and beliefs on her daughter.

Or so Riesling thought.

She also believed that Theo would have gotten bored with being a father and left. She hadn't expected he'd keep coming around for scraps.

"When Ashling was a year old, I moved from Ohio back to New Jersey with custody of my daughter. Theo barely even had visitation, so I never thought he'd come back. But he did. And that's when this vicious cycle started of me giving him money in hopes he'd go away and never come back."

"Until he bled you dry."

She nodded. "That was about seven months ago now. I'm sure he was scoping out where I live and assessing what he thinks I have or what he can hold over me. That's how he operates." She groaned. "And by calling you over, I might have played right into his hands."

Trey took her chin between his thumb and forefinger. "He's not going to be able to come at you through me. That's impossible."

"He'll find your weak spot and exploit it." What had she done? Theo might not look like the brightest bulb in the shed, but he wasn't stupid. He always did his research when it came to the people he scammed. He knew how to play to people's emotions. He'd find the things that hit Trey's heart.

Finding his birth parents.

Theo had always been fascinated by the secrets hidden on The River Winery. He used to tell Riesling they could make a fortune if only they knew what they were. Thankfully, Theo had been run out of town before he could find out what any of them were.

"If he has any idea you're here looking for your—"

Trey pressed his finger over her lips. "Even if Theo came to me with knowledge of where I came from, I'm not going to give him money for it. I want answers, but I'm not desperate for them."

"Are you sure about that? Theo can be incredibly persuasive and you moved here to find out your history. This means a lot to you."

"It does." He nodded. "But Ashling's well-being means more to me." He brushed his lips over Riesling's in a tender kiss. It wasn't passionate, but it was powerful and it made her feel as though things might actually be okay. "To be honest, I'm scared to find my birth parents."

"Why?"

"My father said something to me when I set out on this path that has struck a chord with me and I've never forgotten it."

"What's that?"

"He told me that just because my adoption was illegal,

doesn't mean I was stolen. It could simply mean that those involved went a great deal to keep it a secret and by me coming and looking for answers, I could be opening a box of secrets that could destroy lives all because I was selfish." He smiled weakly. "I still want to know and sometimes I feel guilty about that and it's why I want to be quiet about it. I don't want to hurt anyone in my quest."

"You're a very special man."

"I wouldn't go that far," he whispered.

She wrapped her arms tightly around his shoulders and kissed him, hard, pushing up against the door, losing herself in the moment.

If she were being honest with herself—with her heart—she didn't ever want to let go. A sense of desperation filled her gut. She couldn't get enough of Trey. She grappled at his shirt, tugging, pulling, and twisting. The need to feel his naked body against her skin was too much to bear. She needed him in the most primal way.

"Hey," he said softly. "I'm not sure the middle of your family room with Ashling asleep upstairs is the right place for this."

She took his hand and tugged him up the stairs. "I have a lock on my door."

"I don't—"

"It's fine. How on earth do you think married people with kids do it?"

"I suppose that's a good point." He jumped past her

at the top of the stairs and opened her bedroom door. Once inside, he tugged it closed.

The lock clicked.

Butterflies consumed her belly. She flattened her hand over her stomach. Since she and Theo ended their not-so-great relationship, Riesling hadn't allowed herself to have many short-lived relationships, if she could even call them that.

"You're so beautiful." Trey lifted her shirt over her head and dabbled kisses across her neck and shoulders.

She enjoyed the dark timbre of his voice and the way it tumbled over her skin.

He took his time removing her clothing, making sure every inch of her body was given his full attention. She'd never considered herself a selfish lover. Normally, she just wanted to get it over with. Find a fraction of satisfaction and be done. But tonight, she wanted to linger on the verge of intoxication.

Gently, he laid her on the bed and continued to give her the kind of pleasure she'd been dreaming about.

She sucked in all the feels like a sponge. They moved together like the sand and the sea. He understood her body as well as she did. As soon as she wanted him to touch her a certain way, before she could even express it, he catered to her needs, wants, and desires.

Never had she been with someone who put her above himself.

He kissed a path down her neck, chest, and across her middle.

Staring at him while he kissed her most intimately, her pulse exploded. She thought her heart might pound right out of her chest. She gripped the sheets, digging her heels into the mattress. Her orgasm tore through her body like a tidal wave crashing into the shore. She gasped, unable to fill her lungs with enough oxygen. Frantically, she tried again and again until her climax slowed, settling in her gut, winding down like the tail end of a storm, but she knew another one was brewing on the horizon and she wasn't about to let it get away.

"I want you," she said.

He didn't waste any time and she took him in deep. Arching her back, she clutched his shoulders as another wave sent her body soaring. He took her mouth in a hot, wet kiss. His entire body tensed as he gripped her hips, slamming into her hard and fast.

It was as if the Fourth of July fireworks had erupted between their bodies.

She heaved in a long breath and squeezed her eyes closed. The reality of her feelings smacked her heart.

Trey could hurt her in the worst of ways and she could no longer prevent it from happening. Without even realizing it, she'd entrusted him with her soul.

He rolled to the side and pulled the blanket over their naked bodies. The moonlight shone in through the windowpane, casing a white glow across his sweet face.

She palmed his cheek. She could handle having her heart crushed, but she couldn't tolerate it if he broke Ashling's.

Something she felt the need to make sure he understood now.

She shifted her gaze and palmed his cheek. "I've come to care about you."

He smiled. "I care about you too."

"We're taking a risk because we work together, but we're grown-ups. If or when this ends, I'm sure we can figure it out. But I can't have Ashling as collateral damage."

"I would never do anything to intentionally hurt your daughter. She and I have developed a friendship. I can keep that at whatever level you want me to."

"Thank you. I appreciate that." She snuggled in closer, wrapping her arm and leg around him tighter. "I'm sorry, but you can't sleep here."

"I understand."

She closed her eyes and for a few moments, enjoyed what it was like to be in the arms of a man who cared about what she wanted.

12

RIESLING

When Riesling had asked for a mother-daughter breakfast, she hadn't expected to be asked to start the day before the sunrise so her mother could toss perfectly good items that could be given to Goodwill in random trash receptacles.

"It's awfully nice of Trey to take Ashling this morning and put her on the school bus," her mom said. "He's such a sweet man."

Riesling didn't want to get into this conversation at the crack of dawn with her mother. It was way too early to have that talk. "Mom. Why are you putting those things in the dumpster when we could be having a charity pick them? A lot of them are in good shape."

"So Lyra Chambers can find them and have them. She needs to have some nicer things for her boys and her mother's being a bitch."

"Are you kidding me right now?" Riesling took the old leather office chair that one could consider to be in *mint condition* and tossed it over the edge of the green garbage bin in the back alley of Main Street.

"No. That Clarisse can be one stuck-up woman and the way she's treating her own daughter right now is just shameful."

"Do you not see the irony here?" Riesling laughed. "When I left with Theo, you cut me off. You wouldn't give me a dime, except when it came to Ashling."

"That's entirely different. That boy was bleeding you dry. And let's be honest, you were doing that to spite me. Besides, the first few years you left town, if I gave you something, he'd end up taking it."

Riesling couldn't argue that point. She'd been so hurt and angry that she couldn't bring herself to go home much less ask anyone in her family for help. It didn't help that Theo had scammed a few townspeople for a lot of money. "Why not just give it to Lyra then?"

"Trust me when I say we have to let her go dumpster diving—or whatever it's called—for it. I'm just worried someone will start calling her a *dumpster diving diva* or something if anyone finds out. I mean, that child used to be just like her mother. Poor kid."

Riesling tightened her jaw. "You've never shown me that kind of compassion. Never."

"That's not true." Weezer tossed a few more things into the dumpster and turned, planting her hands on her hips.

Oh shit. Here it comes. There was no stopping her mother when she got like this.

"Yes. I stopped giving you money and things. But I never stopped taking care of you or Ashling. We bought you food. Paid car insurance. Health insurance. We did what we could to make sure you both were being taken care of whenever Theo started draining your savings, because that's all that man has ever done, so don't go pulling that crap with me." Her mother narrowed her glare and stepped closer. "I've supported every decision you've ever made except one." She held up her finger. "And that was to be in a relationship with Theo after he swindled kind, decent people out of all the money they had. That was it for me. I was done. I won't tolerate that and—"

"I didn't tolerate it either, Mother. But he's Ashling's father and she loves him."

"But he doesn't love her and someday, when she's holding the purse strings, he'll start trying to take her money. Is that what you want? Because that's what we want to prevent and that's why we want you to..." Her mother let the words trail off as she blew out a puff of air. "I don't want to fight. I love you, Riesling, and I'm so happy that you're back home where you belong."

"But is it where I belong?" Oh shit. Becoming combative with her mom wasn't always a good thing.

"I believe so." Her mom tossed the last item into the dumpster before climbing behind the wheel of the pickup. "We never wanted you to leave in the first place."

Riesling slid into the passenger seat. Having this conversation felt like it was beating a dead horse, but maybe this time she would finally get the answer her heart needed to forgive and put it all in her rearview mirror. "If that were honestly true, then why give me the ultimatum?"

Her mom turned into the parking lot of the Green Bean. She pushed the gear shift into park and shifted in the driver's seat. "The last time we tried to have a real serious conversation about this topic, we ended up not speaking for an entire month. I don't want that to happen again." She stared her down, expressionless.

God, Riesling hated that look because not only couldn't she tell what her mother was thinking, but there was no sign as to what she was feeling and that's one of the biggest reasons Riesling stayed away.

At least when her mom looked at one of her other six children, she did so with emotion. Or at least that's how Riesling felt.

"Well, I want this resolved because I'm tired of feeling like I don't matter to you." She waved her hand in front of the window. "I think it's sweet what you've done for Lyra. The way her mother's acting over Lyra's divorce and then the fact that Lyra wants to fend for herself is ridiculous."

Riesling's mother reached across the cab of the truck and took her hand. "I should have never asked you to choose between the father of your child and me. If had been in your shoes, I might have done the same thing. I'm sorry."

Riesling gasped. Her mother almost never apologized. And even though her delivery was wrong, she'd been right about Theo all along.

"I'm proud of you," her mother continued. "I wasn't going to say this to you. Your father thought it was better if I stayed out of it and for the most part, I have to agree. All you and I do is butt heads. But I want Theo out of yours and Ashling's life for good. I think you're making a mistake by sitting around and waiting for him to disappear. He's only going to hurt that darling little girl."

"I know," Riesling said. "I'm meeting Dad tonight after his dinner with Jimmy Armstrong."

Her mom tilted her head. "Your father didn't say anything to me about that."

"I asked him not to."

"Why?"

"Because you always judge me and I didn't want to hear about all the reasons why I should have done this years ago."

Her mother squeezed her hand. "Maybe if I hadn't asked you to choose between a man and your family, you could have come home when you left Theo instead of feeling as though all I did was mistreat you. And maybe if you'd come home and asked for our help, we'd have done it in the way you'd asked instead of being sneaky about it." Her mom arched a brow. "We can do that game all morning long. We both made mistakes. Just like me and Malbec with the secret that drove us apart, but what good is that going to do us now?"

"You're right. It's not going to get us anywhere, but I need to know that you're going to let me do this my way." She squeezed her mother's hand. "I'm not exactly sure what that looks like because I don't know how much of a leg I have to stand on and what Theo might do when he's backed into a corner, but I agree. I need to take the necessary steps to be rid of Theo and then always be that safe place for my daughter to land."

"I want to be that for you as well."

A few tears burned in Riesling's eyes. She'd waited years to hear, more importantly feel, those words. "You are, Mom. And I love you."

"I love you too, little girl. I always have and I always will." Her mother reached out and touched her cheek. "So, tell me about you and Trey."

Riesling laughed. Leave it to her mother to go right from an emotional topic to one that Riesling didn't want to talk about. Not yet anyway.

"He's a nice young man. Handsome. Smart. But what the hell is he really looking for and don't lie to me because I'm not buying he's looking for a friend of his."

It wasn't Riesling's story to tell and she wasn't about to break his trust. But she also had made way too much progress with her mother not to give her something, especially since it had been her office he'd been snooping in. "I can't tell you," Riesling said. "And not because I don't want to, but because I'm not sure Trey would want me to. I have to ask him first."

"That's about as honest an answer as I can expect, I guess." Her mother smiled. "You really like him, don't you?"

"I do," she admitted. "But I'm scared."

"About what?"

"That the reason he came to Candlewood Falls is the reason he's going to leave."

Trey

Trey stood at the end of the driveway, holding Ashling's hand while they waited for the school bus.

Never in a million years did he think he'd be doing this. Not even for a friend.

Or someone he wanted to be more than a friend.

He swallowed that thought.

He hadn't planned on staying in Candlewood Falls any longer than it took to find his birth parents. He glanced down at the little girl clutching his fingers.

Ashling looked up at him and smiled wide. "Grandma River is picking me up after school and taking me to dinner and a movie. Just the two of us."

"That sounds like a lot of fun."

Ashling nodded wildly. "Grandma says you and my ma need some alone time, so we need to give you some space."

Trey tried to stifle his laugh. "What gave her that idea?"

"Grandma says you and my mom should be dating, and I agree." Ashling pursed her lips. "But I'm not supposed to be talking to you about it."

"I promise not to tell Weezer or your mom." Trey should nip this conversation in the ass right there and if he saw a yellow bus coming down the street, he would. But since that wasn't happening, he couldn't help himself. "What do you think about me and your mom going out together?"

"You mean like boyfriend and girlfriend?"

He nodded like a big goofy kid. He wondered if his cheeks hurting meant he was smiling like one too. Life had a way of taking people in different directions when they least expected it and his world had turned upside down and sideways after his mother died.

Once he found that note, he never thought he'd be the same. He thought he'd lost his identity. It took some soul searching and a lot of forgiveness for Trey to come to the conclusion that his parents, as selfish as they had been, gave him a good home and lots of love.

And it didn't change who he was at the fundamental level.

Now that he'd lived in Candlewood Falls for a bit

over a month, his world had flipped again. He no longer wished to race back to the city. He wanted to linger in this country life.

With Riesling.

He wanted to explore what a world with her and her daughter would be like. He'd already come clean about his adoption. Now he needed to tell her about his millions.

Not that it should change how she viewed him, but it was more about the secret.

That and how he'd planned on leaving as soon as he found the truth. Both those pieces could ruin any chance he had.

"I thought you were already Mommy's boyfriend," Ashling said.

He bent down, getting on the young girl's level. He took her by the forearms. "Sometimes these things aren't always that cut and dry. Sometimes it takes grown-ups a while to define that kind of relationship. But I care about you and your mom a lot. So, if I don't have your blessing, then I'm not sure it's a good idea."

Ashling took him by the cheeks. "Even Grandma River says you're good for my mom and she doesn't think anyone is good enough for her, especially my daddy." Ashling crinkled her nose and made a strange look with her face as if she'd eaten an entire lemon. "Everyone thinks I'm a baby."

"I don't," Trey said. "You're not an adult, but you're a big girl and smarter than a lot of children your age."

"I am." She nodded. "Can I tell you something?"

"Of course."

"My Grandma River sometimes cries at night over my mommy."

That about damn near broke Trey's heart.

"Why?"

"Grandma River says it's because she made the worst mistake ever when it came to my mama and she hasn't been able to fix it. I overheard Grandpa say he's got a plan and he told Grandma not to worry. That he'll take care of everything, including my daddy."

Trey sucked in a deep breath. That's a lot for a little girl to take in. "What does that mean?"

"I've seen the news," she said softly as she wiped a tear from her cheek. "I know my dad isn't a good person. He takes people's money and doesn't do what he says he's going to. He's a liar. He's lied to me." The little girl squared her shoulders. "All my grandparents and aunts and uncles teach me to forgive. And I try to do that. But my daddy doesn't deserve it. Not anymore and I hope my grandpa's plan works."

"Have you told your mom about any of this?"

Ashling shook her head.

"Why not?" Trey had never been so happy for a school bus to be late.

"My mommy never says a bad thing about anyone. I know Grandma River hurt her feelings real bad once, but she's never said anything but how much my grandma loves us and how she'd move heaven and earth for us. I know that. Mommy doesn't say bad things about my dad. Though she doesn't say nice things, either. And Daddy always manages to make us both cry. I don't want to do that anymore. I was thinking maybe you and I can help my grandpa with his plan. Do you think that's possible?"

Well, shit. He hadn't expected that question. He kissed her forehead. This wasn't even close to being in his wheelhouse. However, he felt confident that he'd know exactly how Riesling would want him to answer, especially if he wanted to remain in her life.

"Because I don't believe you're a baby, I'm going to be honest with you, okay?"

"Okay."

"We need to have a conversation with your mom about this."

Ashling shook her head. "She'll just get upset."

"Trust me on this. She'd rather you tell her about how you feel and all that you know, then have you go behind her back, and I promise I'll be right there with you when you talk to her. We can do it tomorrow. I'll come with your mom when she picks you up. Okay?"

"Do you promise?"

If something happened to force him to break that promise, he'd rip that little girl's heart to shreds. "I don't make promises because sometimes things happen. But what I will tell you is that I will call you if something changes. But I don't plan on there being any reason I can't come with your mom tomorrow to pick you up."

"Deal." She kissed his cheek just as the bus rolled to a stop. "See you tomorrow." She ran up the steps, turning at the top. She waved over her shoulder. "Have a great day!"

13

CARTER

"That's all easy to do, Jimmy." Carter wiped his lips with his napkin and tossed it on his plate. He lifted his wineglass and took a small sip.

"There's more." Jimmy pushed his food aside and rested his elbows on the table. His gaze darted around the room as if he were afraid of who might be glancing in their direction.

Having been the mayor, there were many rumors, stories, and discussions about Jimmy over the years, but he never cared. He and his wife always held their heads high and acted as though it never fazed them. His wife told the world that it was expected and that the entire town would prefer to find dirt on them rather than spend time on the real issues of the town.

Because of their attitude, they were two of the highest respected people in Candlewood Falls.

Only, there was a tarnish on their marriage and Carter knew it.

"What do you mean?" Carter asked. "The changes in your will aren't difficult. I can have it redrafted and before Christmas."

"That's wonderful, considering that's right around the corner. I really appreciate it. But I want a letter attached to my will to only be read by the recipient. I don't want my wife or children to know."

This damn letter again. It was going to be the death of Carter.

"You mentioned this the last time I drafted your will five years ago, but you never gave it to me or told me what it was about. As your lawyer, anything you put in writing, even if it's going to be read after your death, I should take a look at."

Jimmy pulled an envelope out of his breast coat pocket. He set it down on the table, but with the writing facedown. He kept a protective hand over it. "As my lawyer, anything I tell you, it must be kept confidential."

"I'm well aware of that." Carter lifted his wineglass and swirled. The last time they had this conversation, Jimmy had changed his mind. He'd decided he couldn't tell anyone. That he couldn't risk anyone finding out.

Carter could understand that fear, even if he didn't know what the hell the old man was talking about.

But Carter wasn't an idiot. He had an idea.

"I never want anyone to find out about this letter

except for the recipient. Which means I'd need you to deliver it and express my wishes."

Carter tuned out the noise in the restaurant and focused on his long-time client and friend. He honestly had no problem doing that, but only if he knew what he was getting into. He suspected and that brought him to the young man walking into the diner with his daughter.

The first piece of the puzzle had come together when Trey had asked questions about Allison and Armstrong.

But the rest of it fell into place between Trey getting caught snooping and this moment.

Trey Jefferson looked way too much like Jimmy Armstrong when he'd been a young man.

Worse, Carter could see a little bit of Janet Sprouse in Trey. Hell. He could see more than a little.

The good citizens of Candlewood Falls stopped talking about if Janet and Jimmy were having an affair when Jimmy had been elected the second time. Jimmy's wife put an end to that. However, five months later, Janet left town in what seemed like the middle of the night. No one heard from her for three years until she showed up a few towns away.

Married.

It was rare that she ever stepped foot in Candlewood Falls and the rumor mill spun its ugly web, all centered around Janet's father and his cheating ways and that Janet had simply had enough of her dad.

Honestly, the first person that Carter had thought about when it came to giving up kids and using an illegal adoption ring had been Albert, Janet's father. That was still possible.

"What does the letter say?" Carter asked.

"I have your word this stays right here?"

"I've never broken your confidence. I won't start now," Carter said.

"There are only two other people who know about this and one of them is dead. But I worry that it will come out anyway, especially after what happened to you and Weezer with the winery. I'm thinking by doing this, I can protect my children." Jimmy pushed the envelope across the table. "All of my kids."

Carter took the white paper and lifted it.

Treyton Jefferson.

Fuck. Carter glanced around. His back was to the wall in the corner booth, so no one could see the words on the page, but still. Trey sat at the bar across the room.

Obviously, Jimmy hadn't seen them come in, or he might have thought twice about having this conversation in a public place.

"What is this?" Carter asked.

"I'm not going to say it out loud. Not here. Just read it."

"Why didn't we do this in my office?" Carter fiddled with the edge of the envelope. He wasn't sure he wanted to read the note, especially with what he was going to have to say next.

"We always discuss business here and if I changed that, my wife would become suspicious." He waggled his finger at the piece of paper that Carter unfolded. "She knows and she doesn't want me doing this. But I have to. I need to. I've wanted to do it for thirty-five years."

Dear Treyton,

I don't know what you've been told about your adoption and I'm sorry you've had to learn about me after I've passed away, but I couldn't come to you and tell you for a lot of reasons. I didn't want to hurt your family or mine. I know that's selfish of me and cowardly, but I also promised your birth mother I would respect her wishes, even though it's not what I wanted.

You see, I was married and having an affair with your mom, a younger woman. Oh. I was so much in love with Janet, your birth mom. I thought she loved me too, so when I found out she was pregnant, I thought we'd find a way to make it work. I knew that leaving my wife would end my career. I could even lose my other kids, but people survive divorce and even betrayal.

And you needed your parents.

However, your mother, who really is a good person, said she didn't love me and told me she had no plans on keeping you. Because her father was notorious for having one affair after the other, and the shame she felt it brought on her family, she didn't want the same for herself, so I went to a doctor I knew who had helped a few others in our situation. He promised to find you a good home.

I made sure I knew where you went because I needed to know. I paid extra for that information.

I'm sorry. It sounds like I sold you and maybe I did.

Carter couldn't read another word. He didn't have to. He folded the paper and stuffed it back into the envelope. He reached for his wine and gulped it in two swallows.

"I need to tell you something." Carter let out a long breath as he ran a hand across his face. "My daughter, Riesling, is dating Trey."

"I knew they were working together, but I didn't know that part."

"There's more." Carter didn't like breaking confidences, but Jimmy needed to be somewhat prepared. Carter tapped the letter. "This is not the way to tell Trey. And you can't wait until you're dead. That could be ten years or more." Between dealing with Theo, and now all this, things could get ugly, and Carter needed to keep it all under control. He needed to manage it for his family. They had come too far for it all to blow up now. "He's searching for you."

Jimmy's eyes grew wide. His jaw dropped open. "How do you know?"

"He came to us pretending to search for a friend, but I know better," Carter admitted. "And I have reason to believe that Doctor Allison might have hidden all the adoption records on my land." Carter held up his hand.

"I don't know that for a fact and I'm asking you not to repeat that. My wife would kill me. I need to find it."

"You're searching for it?"

Carter nodded. He hadn't told anyone he'd started digging. He nearly laughed out loud at the obscurity of him sneaking out in the middle of the night, like Weezer's grandfather, but after all that he'd learned, especially after this conversation, he knew buried beneath the surface were all the secrets. He just had to find them. "I promised the boy I'd help and he's pieced a lot of this together. Please don't turn around, but he's at the bar with Riesling and he's waiting to talk to you."

"Me? About what?" Jimmy snatched the letter and stuffed it in his pocket. "There is no way he could know I'm his..." Jimmy's voice trailed off. "What does he want?"

"To talk to you about Doctor Allison and if it was possible he was running an illegal adoption ring."

"I was the mayor at the time. If I admitted—"

"Jimmy. Bigger picture here," Carter interrupted. "He's not here to put anyone in jail or report anyone. Hell, how Weezer didn't know about any of this is beyond me, but all Trey wants is clues so he can find his birth parents. He only wants to know where he came from."

Jimmy lowered his head. He swiped at his cheeks. "Imagine my surprise when I heard that young man was going to be our doctor. I've been in complete shock ever since. So much so that I'm looking at property in Florida."

"You've been talking about getting out of the cold for good for a few years now."

Jimmy lifted his gaze. "I never wanted to give him up. When Janet insisted, I thought about adopting him myself. I even went to Nadine and asked her if she wanted to adopt a baby. That I knew of a situation, but Nadine isn't stupid. She knew we'd be taking my child. She said no."

"Nadine knows about his existence?"

"She knows I had another child, but she doesn't know who he is. After I realized Janet never loved me and I committed fully to making my marriage work, Nadine and I never spoke about it again, but I couldn't ever let it go and I kept up with Trey." Jimmy spoke so softly it was hard to hear him, but Carter appreciated the man's honesty.

However, it was the tears that broke Carter's heart. It was obvious that Jimmy had never forgotten about the son he'd given up.

Or that he'd loved him.

Still loved him.

"I knew about every broken bone, about medical school, about his failed marriage. I felt like I was part of his life, even though I wasn't, which was made apparent when he showed up here." Jimmy shook his head. "I can't talk to him right now. I can't. I'm sorry. Please give him my apologies. Tell him my wife needed me home or something. Anything." Jimmy stood and tossed a bunch of cash on the table. "Thanks for taking care of my will. I'll be in touch."

Trey

Trey followed Riesling into the local bar and tavern. Their talk with Ashling had gone well enough. Riesling hadn't been shocked, considering Ashling had mentioned a few things the night before.

But the poor kid was only six. And as brilliant as the child was, her brain couldn't put all the pieces together the same way an adult could, making it impossible for her comprehend all the details.

The truly hard part had been asking Ashling to continue to keep her feelings to herself with everyone in the family until Grandpa Richardson and Grandpa River's plan was put into place and that little girl had a million and one questions about whatever that plan might be and how she could be of service, but she finally agreed it was best if she let the grown-ups take care of adult things and she continue to be a kid.

What mattered was she wasn't going to have to worry about it anymore. No one was going to force her to see her father again. Not unless she wanted to and she made it clear, she did not.

He wiggled his fingers. Taking in a deep breath, he let all the scents from the dinner assault his nose. Grease. Meat sizzling on a grill. Bacon. His favorite. Who didn't love bacon. Butter and warm bread with a hint of garlic. His stomach reacted with a big growl.

Pressing his hand on Riesling's hip, he guided her into the main room and glanced around. He had a list of questions for Jimmy Armstrong and he'd been playing them in his mind for the last few hours. But now that he was moments away from his first big break, everything he wanted to know seemed to have escaped his brain.

"Relax. You're acting like a jittery, scared cat," Riesling said.

What had surprised Trey the most about Riesling was that after everything she'd been through with her mom, she was still willing to keep his secret about why he wanted to press Jimmy Armstrong about his affair.

That took guts especially after her mom had made two comments earlier about how some things are better off left alone, especially when one is committed to being completely honest.

However, he was willing to let the cat out of the bag.

But only if he knew he was headed down the right path. It wasn't that he had issues with the world knowing he was adopted. Hell, that was something that most people knew. But he thought if Armstrong knew Trey was on the hunt for himself, he might not be so willing to share information.

"Any tips on how to handle Armstrong?" Trey asked. He had no idea why he'd developed such nerves. All he was going to do was have a discussion with an older gentleman about Doctor Alison and some possible discrepancies he'd found in some old records.

Total lie since all the files in his office had all the i's dotted and t's crossed and nothing indicated illegal adoptions, much less legal ones. He was beginning to wonder how important finding his birth parents really was to him anymore. Of course, he spent every waking moment, that he wasn't with Riesling or her daughter, at the library or going through all the information in his office, but he found nothing useful at all.

"Just be yourself and ask your questions. Jimmy likes to talk," she said quickly. "My father is expecting me. I told him that you and I had a date and—"

"We're on a date?"

She glanced over her shoulder and narrowed her stare. "If you play your cards right, you might get lucky. So, yeah. It could be considered a date." She held up her finger. "But only if you play your cards right and as of right now, the first hand didn't go your way."

"They call me the comeback kid." He rested her hand on the small of her back. "And maybe all I'll need is my charm."

She patted his cheek. "Aw. Look at you being all confident about having that effect on me."

"Sometimes you're not that great for my ego."

"Until I call out your name in the middle of wild, passionate—"

"Don't say that out loud when your father is in the same room." When he'd first met his ex-wife, they used to have fun together and a lot of it, but the moment she found out the kind of money he came from, things changed. She'd become distant, as if she no longer had interest in him sexually. It was all about the things, not the romance. Except, he was expected to bring her expensive gifts if he was going to get any attention.

Yeah. That didn't work for him.

Ever since his ex-wife, he'd chosen to keep parts of himself under wraps. There were still things about Trey that Riesling didn't know. He wanted to believe she was the kind of woman that money wouldn't change the way she looked at him or thought about the way he should live his life. Granted, he had a fat bank account, but much of it wouldn't be his until his father passed away. But what he did have, he chose not to spend.

Except for on his business.

However, even that, he wanted to be self-contained.

But it was the idea he hadn't planned on staying in Candlewood Falls that made me think he might have already lost his chance at any kind of future with Riesling. He needed to clear that up with her, tonight.

He pointed to two empty seats at the bar as they passed Jimmy Armstrong and her father.

Trey did a double take. His heart jumped to his throat. He'd seen pictures of Jimmy and there'd been something vaguely familiar about the man. But that had been wishful thinking on Trey's part. All his research between the library and the history book suggested only one man who might have given up a child during the decade that Trey had been born.

But there hadn't been any proof of that and Weezer only agreed to give up the name of the woman who *might have been sleeping* with Armstrong if Trey had the conversation first. That said, Trey's birth father could have been someone who came to Allison from New York. Or Connecticut. Or even Vermont for that matter.

He waved the bartender over and ordered a couple of drinks. Standing behind Riesling, he rested his free hand on her shoulder and rubbed her neck with his thumb. "Are you sure you don't want to wait for me to talk to your dad about his and Harry's plan?"

"Nope. I appreciate the support. But I need to do that on my own." She leaned in and kissed his cheek. "Besides, you're doing that to avoid talking to Armstrong."

"Aren't you the smart one?"

"I hadn't seen it before, but you kind of look like him."

Trey swallowed. Riesling wasn't lying. He'd noticed

the resemblance too, but couldn't bring himself to even think about it outside of the eyes.

"It's subtle, but you have the same jawline," she continued. "And—"

"Could you please stop talking about it?" He took his beer and chugged. "When I was going through the history books and looking at the people who lived here or all the famous people who visited here during the decade I was born, I was always looking at features and wondering if they could be mine. He's not the only one I've seen similarities to." But he certainly was the one who stood out the most.

"Shit," she whispered. "Jimmy's leaving."

Trey swallowed his heartbeat. "What?" He glanced toward the door and watched as the man whom he believed held all the answers walked out the door.

14

RIESLING

The last week had been shitty in general. Mostly because Trey had been walking around in a bad mood, although Riesling couldn't blame him since Jimmy Armstrong and his wife up and left town for a spontaneous vacation, leaving Trey with more questions than answers and her father wouldn't tell him a fucking thing.

Something else she understood, but her father knew more than he was letting on. She could tell by the way he squirmed in his seat. He didn't lie as well as her mother. However, her mom hadn't been much better, avoiding Trey as if she didn't like him, which wasn't true.

Everyone in Riesling's family enjoyed Trey's company so much that she wondered if they preferred to be around him more than her.

Riesling sat at her mother's dining room table with

both her parents and Harry. It was rare that they were all together, but it was time to put an end to Theo's control over her life.

"I don't want him to try to pay me back," Riesling said. "I want him out of my life."

"You're going to have to take him to court." Her father pushed a legal document in front of her. "This is requesting he give up all parental rights. It's not easy to force someone to do it, but Harry and I agree our first course of action should be to ask Theo to walk away without a fight."

"He's not going to do that." Riesling lifted the thick packet. She thought medical terms were hard to understand, but legal contracts where full of language that seemed to be overkill. "Not unless you grease his palms and if you do that, he'll take that as a reason to come back for more. Trust me. It's how I got him down to visitation on my terms."

"I'm aware," her father said. "Harry and I decided to pool some money together. Our only concern is that it will help him get out of his current mess."

Riesling tapped the pen on the table. "Is there any news about what's going on with him? Has anyone seen him?"

"It's not good," Harry said. "He's tried to reach out a couple of times, telling us it's all bogus and asking for help. We won't give it to him."

"So, the plan is to tell him you'll give him money

and help legally with his problems, if he gives up his rights to Ashling."

"On the surface, yes."

"I want to know where you got a hundred grand," she said.

"The where isn't important." Her father pushed his chair back and stood.

It was rare that he paced. "However, knowing Theo, that's not going to stop him, and even though Ashling has been vocal in her feelings, she's still a little girl and if he showed up, he could easily manipulate her into believing he's changed and she wants to spend time with him."

"You're not giving your granddaughter enough credit," Trey said, standing in the middle of the doorway. "I'm sorry. I didn't mean to eavesdrop. I was walking by to get some water before going back out into the vineyard."

Her father folded his arms across his chest.

Riesling swallowed. Her father had always been the kinder, gentler parent, but if you pushed him too far, watch out. He could be worse than The Weezer.

"I doubt that, son," her father said. "I know how smart Ashling is, but she's got her mother's heart."

"I will agree with you on that point." Trey leaned against the doorjamb. "I know this is really none of my business and I'm supposed to be outside digging, but what you're putting on the table isn't enough."

Her father tilted his head and lowered his chin.

Never a good sign.

"It's the most money we've ever offered," her father said. "It's enough to help him get a little bit lost."

"Not really," Trey said. "We all know that Theo did the things he was accused of. We've seen the news coverage and we've seen the authorities looking for him. He knows he's screwed if he shows his face. His only hope is a shit ton of money."

"That's what we're hoping," she said. "Trust me. He'll take whatever he can get."

"Well, I hate to see any of you lose a single penny to that asshole ever again. I think there's a better way to get rid of him once and for all."

"And what would you propose?" her father asked.

"A sting operation," Trey said. "Men like Theo, they like to brag."

"He's right about that," Harry said. "Anytime my son thought he was about to hit it big, he was calling home left and right telling us how he'd finally hit the big leagues. He'd drop names and talk about how he had millions in the bank. He'd even show us pictures of the things he planned on buying Ashling."

"He bought her a few things once. On credit. I was mortified when they all had to be returned. Just like when we got kicked out of the big house on the river in Ohio," Riesling said with a sigh. "That was the final straw for me."

Trey stepped into the dining room, rested his hand on her shoulder, and gave it a good squeeze. "He's driven by money and power and how that makes him look and feel. I grew up with guys like that. It's all that matters to them and no offense, but what you're offering isn't going to be enough to entice him to come out and play. Not when he's looking at real jail time. He needs a couple of million to make it worthwhile."

"Sounds like you've been doing some research on my son," Harry said with a narrowed stare.

"I'm sorry. Again, I mean no disrespect, but my own personal project took a really weird turn and for the last week I've been waiting patiently for someone to tell me the truth." He glanced between her and her father. "I decided to focus my energies on helping Riesling."

"And here I thought you were simply sulking," Riesling said. "You need to respect my father's decision just like he respected yours when we caught—"

"I'm not here to argue," Trey said, locking gazes with her as if not a single other soul was in the room. "I get Carter is protecting his client, as he should. I find that incredibly honorable and I'd like that in a lawyer and a friend. I just find it silly that we all know the truth and instead of speaking it, I'm out there digging for it." Trey held up his hand. "My ex-wife was so into money and prestige it was ridiculous. It's what destroyed our marriage."

"I'm sure being in medical school and then residency wasn't easy on any relationship," her father said.

"That was only part of it." He dropped his hand to

his side and lifted his gaze. "I've always wondered if anyone in this town put my name with my father's."

Harry raised his hand. "I have, but what does being the son of Andrew Jefferson have to do with anything?"

"Andrew Jefferson," her father whispered. "Why do I know that name?"

"He owns a national media company," Harry said.

"Actually, it was my father's news program that broke the story about Theo."

Riesling's stomach flipped. And flopped. "Why didn't you tell me?"

"At first, it had to do more with not wanting people to make judgments about me because of who my father was and his bank account. My ex-wife did that and the moment she found out I had more access than what I had let on, she was spending left and right. She believed I owed it to her."

"Are you saying you're some secret wealthy man?" Riesling honestly didn't care about money, or how much Trey had.

But she did care about being honest, and Trey once again had broken that trust.

"My father is rich. I have a trust fund. I don't like to touch it. I figure it's there for when I have kids of my own someday." He raised his hand again. "But I've seen what money does to people and I don't want that to ever be me. Or anyone I'm with. So I choose to live within my means. Maybe I won't someday, but this has nothing to do with what I think we should do in order to get Theo out of our lives for good."

Riesling's heart pounded. What gave Trey the right to say *we* and *our*?

"I have the money to entice Theo. We use it to get him to come to us to discuss the situation. We tell him he has to give up Ashling. But in the process, we use my father's connections with the media and the authorities to nail the bastard. That way, he doesn't get any money, he goes to jail, and we don't ever have to worry about him again."

"I like that plan," her father said. "But I can't ask you to do it."

"You're not asking. I'm offering," Trey said.

"What is it that you want in return?" her father asked.

"Nothing." Trey had the nerve to smile at her as if he meant it.

"That's bullshit." She bolted out of her chair. "Of course you want something or why else would you keep this from me?"

"Excuse me?" Trey jerked his head back.

She should have known the second she didn't think the other shoe was going to drop, they all fell from the sky. "You acted like we didn't have the money to do things around the office. You acted like my salary was a great big ouch in your bank account."

"The business has to pay for itself or what's the

point," Trey said with a confused look on his face. "Besides, I wanted to do all this without my father's money. I thought you of all people would understand the importance of being independent."

Even though she couldn't argue with that point, she wasn't willing to concede. "You lied to me. You know how I feel about that."

"Yeah, well, both you and your dad know exactly who my birth parents are, and yet you won't say a word. That's a form of lying, but I'm trying to respect your reasons. You need to respect mine."

She glared at Trey. A million thoughts raced through her brain, but only one stuck out.

He never had any intention of staying in Candlewood Falls. If he had, he would have done a lot more to make his practice a success.

She grabbed the pen off the table and signed the papers. "Take the bastard to court. Without this asshole's money."

Trey

"Hey, Dad. How are you?" Trey set his cell on the wine crate.

"Where the hell are you?"

"In the building that used to be Doctor Allison's office on The River Winery."

"I wish you'd give that up," his father said.

"I can't. I think I found my birth father. But I can't be sure." Trey ran a hand across his unshaved face.

"I see." His father glanced down at his folded hands. "Do you want to tell me about him?"

"If you want to know, I'll fill you in as soon as I have the proof, which is why I'm out here digging in the almost frozen ground."

"What the hell are you doing that for?"

"Riesling and her family believe the doctor hid the adoption records out here so we're looking."

"They are helping you?"

Trey nodded.

"You look tired, son."

"I am," he admitted. "I need your help with something."

"What?"

Ever since Trey had found out about the illegal adoption, he and his father had struggled to piece their relationship back together. But he loved his dad and he wasn't about to lose him over this. Thankfully, the more time passed, the more supportive his dad became. Trey did his best to let his father know he wasn't searching to replace him, or that he hadn't felt loved his entire life, because he wouldn't have wanted to trade in his childhood for anything.

"What do you know about the case against a man named Theo Richardson?"

"A lot. Why?" His father's demeanor perked up.

"The girl I've been sort of dating here, that's her daughter's biological father."

"Shit, son. That man is a real jerk. He's swindled millions from good people. I've got my best reporter on this case, but so far, the authorities can't find him. That said, the company he worked for is being picked apart. I wouldn't be surprised if in the next week it's shut down because it's a pyramid scheme. Once that happens, the cops will have all they need to indict Theo. I hope this young lady isn't too involved with him."

"No. As a matter of fact, she's trying to make sure he's out of her life and their daughter's for good. She wants to take him to court, but this is where I need your help, especially if you have an inside track on when all this is going to happen."

"I do, but I have to be careful. I can't mess with what the cops are doing," his father said.

"I wouldn't want you to. But he's staying some-where near Candlewood Falls and I know how to get him to come out and play."

"How?"

"Offer him a few million dollars to give up his parental rights."

His father opened his mouth, but said nothing. He cleared his throat. "Do you hear yourself?"

"I do. I get the hypocrisy."

"As long as you can see it."

Trey nodded. "Will you help me?"

"I'd love to."

15

RIESLING

Riesling wanted to stay mad at Trey forever, but she knew that would be impossible. She absolutely understood why he hadn't said anything about his money. If she were in his shoes, she would have done the same thing. Being rich wasn't something you blurted out in casual conversation, especially considering his past.

And if she was being honest with herself, he hadn't been that stingy when it came to the practice. No. He'd been frugal and was working within the means of their collective income. That was just being smart. Not to mention he'd been using his own money to help Koontz and his daughter. Trey didn't have to do that.

Being wealthy wasn't something that anyone should brag about, a lesson she'd learned from Clarisse Chambers. All that mattered to that woman was what people thought and how she was perceived.

Poor Lyra and her boys.

Riesling could only hope that the things that she and her mom had tossed were helpful to Lyra. That and the rumor mill was all abuzz about Brad Wilde taking a liking to Lyra and her boys. That put warmth in Riesling's heart, but it didn't change her own situation.

"You are deep in thought, dear," her mother said as she moved about the back kitchen in the winery. "I wish you wouldn't worry so much. Everything is going to be okay. Your father, Harry, and now Trey and his father are all involved. We're going to make sure Theo gets what he deserves."

"I hope you're right, Mom." Riesling leaned against the counter. "I just want to make sure my daughter doesn't pay a high price."

"We're all here for you."

If anyone were to ask Riesling even a year ago if she'd be able to spend this much time with her mom, much less feel this close, she would have told that person they'd lost their mind. However, her mother had been nothing but kind and supportive ever since she'd returned.

"How long do you think all this is going to take?" Riesling asked.

Her mother set a pot of water on the stove, then she pulled down two thermoses. "If what Trey's father said is true, it will be over before your brother's wedding."

"I can't believe it's almost Christmas."

"I can't believe Brad Wilde had a child and no one, not even his sister, knew anything about it."

"Yeah. That one was a real shocker." But after seeing Brad with his little girl, Riesling hoped they'd find their way to a good relationship. One that was more than holidays.

"Have you seen what Lacey Wilde has done with the Candlelight Inn?"

"Not yet. But Trey and I are supposed to go on the Victorian Christmas Tour, though he's barely speaking to me and I can't say I've been too communicative with him. We work great together, but the day ends and I come and get Ashling and he doesn't pop over like he used to."

Her mother held up a packet of cocoa and some marshmallows. "I want you to bring this to him and give him a hand."

"Thanks, Mom. I do need to talk to him."

"Ya think?" Her mother shook her head like she did anytime she'd been disappointed.

Riesling was so tired of the family judgments, and she'd been hoping they were past that, but maybe not.

"You do owe him an apology, but he owes you one too and don't let him forget that."

"Oh my. Who are you and what have you done with The Weezer?" When her mother wanted something to happen, like a relationship with one of her kids, she did whatever it took to force it, like manipulating Malbec to believe she was going to sell the winery to

Eliza Jane, when that was the furthest thing from the truth.

So the fact that she agreed Trey might have been wrong and saw Riesling's side of things threw her for a loop.

Her mother smiled. "I think Trey is perfect for you, much like I knew Eliza Jane was the one for Malbec."

"Mom. I've only known him a little over a month."

"It doesn't matter. When it's right, it's right. However, the two of you have a lot going on. There's all this shit with Theo and of course, Trey wants answers about his biology and once we dig up that box, we can tell him."

"Mom. Why can't you tell him what you know now?"

"Because I don't know anything and before you go on about your dad, he hasn't told me what Armstrong said during that meeting and he won't. He's never broken client confidentiality. And he never will. It's why everyone in this town trusts him considering he's married to me."

"But you're not a gossip."

Her mother laughed. "I wasn't always like that. I learned my lesson the hard way."

The teakettle whistled. Her mom lifted it and poured it into two large mugs. "I will give you this, because I know it's important to Trey and I trust him." Her mother twisted the tops onto the thermoses. "Jimmy Armstrong and his wife are back in town."

"What? When? How do you know?"

"I heard it at the salon," her mother said. "Nadine couldn't stand to be away for the Victorian Christmas Tour and told her husband that he better bring her back, or she was coming back without him. They have been holed up in their house, preparing for it."

"How are they keeping it a secret?"

"They really aren't." Her mother inched closer and took her by the forearms. "Make things right with Trey."

"Guess I better go apologize and talk him into going on that date tomorrow night."

Her mother palmed her cheek. "I like Trey. He's a good man. I know you're worried he came here only to find his birth parents and then leave, and maybe that's the truth, but if you want him, fight for him."

"Wait a second. Are you telling me you're not going to go meddling in my love life?"

Her mother laughed. "I didn't say that." She lowered her chin. "I'm going to work my good old Weezer charm on that boy until he couldn't leave this town if he tried."

"Please don't." Riesling kissed her mother's cheek. "Let me work mine, okay?"

"If you need backup, let me know."

Riesling bundled herself up and carried the two thermoses out to the overflow building, surprised that Trey wasn't outside digging, but inside moving shelves around.

Trey had dug three holes about two feet deep. Currently, he stood in front of a fourth one as he pushed the shovel into the ground and stomped on it. "This is the fucking dumbest thing I've ever done," he said as he glanced up, catching her gaze. "And yet, here I am, hoping that every time I put this damn thing in the dirt, I'm going to hit some magic lamp or something."

She laughed.

"It's not funny."

"Visualizing you rubbing a lamp in hopes a genie might—"

"That's not what I meant." He took the mug from her hands and twisted the top. "Your father swears that your grandpa always dug close to the building."

"My dad wouldn't send you on a wild goose chase."

"But he knows Armstrong is my father. Why won't he just confirm it for me?"

"He'd lose his ability to practice law."

"It was a rhetorical question." Trey adjusted his hat and took a long sip of his cocoa. "I'm sorry. I don't mean to be so moody. I'm just frustrated. I can't be the only one looking for their birth parents only to hit a brick wall. I mean, I know for a fact that Doctor Allison helped my father's friend when he got his mistress pregnant."

"Well, I've got some news that might brighten your day." She found a log and sat down. "The Armstrongs have returned and will be showcasing their house at the Victorian Christmas Tour."

"How is that going to help me?"

"Jimmy and Nadine always greet the guests. He'll have to engage with you, especially if I'm on your arm." She raised her hot chocolate. "It's not the best way to create dialogue, but it will force the issue."

"I'm not sure I want to do it like that." He sat next to her, pressing his leg against hers, and stared into her eyes. "I'm sorry I've been a bit of a dick these last few days. It's not you I'm upset with. It's the entire situation."

"I know." She tried to keep from smiling. The fact he came right out and tried made all the difference in the world. But that didn't solve the issue. "I haven't helped any by the way I've treated you. I wasn't mad that you didn't tell me about who your dad was or that you had money. I'm scared over what all that means." She had no idea how to bring this up. They'd been seeing each other, if you could call it that, for maybe a month and a half. It wasn't even a relationship yet.

Though she cared for him in ways she wasn't sure were possible. She'd been so wrapped up in taking care of Ashling and trying to keep Theo at bay that she'd never allowed herself to feel much of anything for any man she spent time with.

But Trey was different.

"I need to ask you something and I'm begging you

to be honest with me," she said, staring at the thermos in her hands.

"Okay."

She sucked in a deep breath and let it out slowly, counting to ten. She tried not to think about the answer she didn't want to hear. The one that meant he'd be leaving Candlewood Falls most likely by spring. "When you bought this practice, was it about being a doctor in a small town? Or was it all about finding your birth parents and this illegal adoption thing?"

He shifted in his seat, turning to face her head-on. He set his mug between his feet. "That's a loaded question."

"I don't see how."

"The truth is when I first came here, my only reason was to find answers. But I knew it could take months. Maybe even a year and I needed to work. So—"

"You bought Harden's practice with the idea to make it profitable to sell it when you got the information you desired."

"Yes," he said matter-of-factly.

"I thought as much." She stood.

He jumped to his feet. "A lot has changed since I moved here." Trey took her mug and set it on the stump before taking her into his arms.

She gasped, taking a step back, but he didn't let her go. He held her tighter, drawing her to his chest.

"I never thought I was cut out for small-town life. It seemed so boring. You should have seen me the first time I walked down Main Street and everyone here looked me in the eye and said hello. Totally freaked me out. No one in the city does that."

"I know. It's why I hate going there for the most part."

Trey chuckled. "I'm not sure I'll enjoy going back."

Riesling's heart dropped to the pit of her gut. He hadn't said he was going back, but he didn't say he wasn't either.

"I like living in Candlewood Falls. I like being a doctor here." He leaned in and brushed his mouth across hers in a tender kiss. "I really like you and before we made headway on who my birth parents were, I was questioning why I wanted to go back to the city when I could have a really nice life here."

Her pulse raced. This was exactly what she wanted to hear, but she couldn't trust it. It was too soon. He could easily go running back to New York the second things got real.

And they would. He was dating a woman with a six-year-old daughter. That alone would have a set of challenges that would send any normal man running when that child wasn't their responsibility.

Not to mention the issues with Theo, which weren't resolved.

And, of course, the illegal adoption ring that had yet to be cracked.

"I like you too, but—"

He pressed his finger against her lips. "There are no

guarantees in life and while I had every intention of leaving when I first got here, that's not what I want now."

She swallowed. "You don't plan on selling the practice as soon as you get confirmation?"

He ran his thumb across her cheek. "No. I want to see where things go with you and Ashling. That is if you still want to date me?"

"Please don't lie to me anymore, okay?"

He kissed her nose. "I need you to not take advantage of my father's money. I won't use it just because it's there. It's important to me that I make it on my own. That my business pays for itself and that—"

She kissed him. Hard. Hoping that she didn't need to answer or explain anything else. She became dizzy in his embrace. At one point, she'd thought she'd been in love with Theo, but all that had been was lust, lies, and a way to push her mother's buttons. She hadn't realized that back then she'd felt left out of the family, which had been by choice. She wasn't into making wine. She didn't have a talent for it and her sales skills like the twins and Zinfandel were pathetic.

All she ever wanted to do was help people.

In her quest to find herself, she'd gotten lost in Theo's lies.

Now she found herself lost in a man who might not have told her everything about himself the moment they met, but when it counted, he was honest.

And he was present.

He gripped her by the biceps and took a step back. "As much as I could stand here and kiss you all night, it's getting late and I want to dig a little longer."

"Is there another shovel?" she asked.

"There sure is. Malbec was out here earlier helping. He asked me if I was coming to the wedding. As your date."

"What did you tell him?"

"That you hadn't asked me yet, but if you did, I'd say yes."

"Wow. You've been taking lessons from my mother on how to get your way." She laughed.

"Are you asking?"

"I might be." She took the shovel and dug it into the ground. It banged, hard, against something. She glanced at Trey. "Holy shit. I think I found something."

Trey

Trey stared at the wooden coffin buried in the ground while he waited for Riesling and her father. Trey had promised he wouldn't open it until Carter arrived and he'd stick to his word. He owed that to Riesling.

But holy crap, a fucking coffin?

It's not like Trey had never seen a dead body before.

He'd had worked on his share of cadavers during medical school and it had never bothered him.

Not one bit.

But if there was a body in that wooden box, he might freak out just a little bit.

The sound of boots hitting the hard ground caught his attention. He glanced up to see Riesling, her father, and her mother racing in his direction.

"We heard you found something," Carter said.

"You could say that." Trey pointed to the box in the ground. It wasn't a fancy coffin that one might buy at a funeral home for their loved one. It was more like something that a person made at the last minute when they had no money and only needed to put a person—or something else—into the ground.

"Why don't I help you lift that sucker out of that hole," Carter said.

"Sounds good to me." Trey leaned forward and gripped the top part of the box while Carter did the same at the other end. "On the count of three."

Carter nodded.

"One. Two. Three." Trey braced himself, preparing for it to be incredibly heavy. However, when he lifted the box, it certainly didn't hold the weight of a human body. He set it on the ground and let out a long breath. "There's no way a person is buried in that thing unless they were under fifty pounds."

"Well, let's find out what's actually in there," Weezer said with her hands planted on her hips.

"I can't look." Riesling turned and faced the other way. "I don't care how many corpses I've seen, I've never dug one up."

Trey opted not to make a snide comment. He wanted to keep his date for both the Victorian Christmas Tour and Malbec's wedding.

But more importantly, he wanted to show Riesling that he understood her and was willing to be by her side, no matter what.

He used the peen side of the hammer to pry open the coffin while Carter used his cell as a flashlight. It took only five minutes to shimmy the top aside.

"Papers," Trey said. "It's just papers. No dead body." He dropped to his knees and stuck his hands into the wood box. He lifted a file and let it drop open on his lap. "Jesus." He stared at what looked like a young mother's records. He flipped through the pages, finding information about the birth and potential adoptive parents. "This is it." He glanced up, catching Riesling's gaze. "All this is Allison's records. The proof of who my parents are is in this coffin."

16

RIESLING

Riesling stepped off the school bus at the Candlelight Inn. So far, the adventure had been more like a high school reunion for her brother Malbec and his buddies Brad and Caleb.

But she relished in the light-hearted teasing. It was much needed after they'd dug up a coffin full of illegal adoption records.

The worst part had been that Doctor Allison had used The River Winery address on all his correspondence, linking the winery to his illegal operation.

If they turned over the documents to the authorities, it could ruin the winery. If they didn't, could Trey continue to live with himself? Because he'd be covering up a horrible lie.

Of course, her mother and father were calling all the shots. It was their property and they wanted a few days to verify all the information they'd found, and they also wanted Trey to have a conversation with his biological father.

Before Christmas.

Which was only a few days away.

After the holiday passed, they would collectively sit down and have a conversation about what to do with the evidence that could destroy everything the River family had worked so hard to protect.

"Come on." Riesling tugged at Trey's arm.

"This is the weirdest thing I've ever done," Trey whispered. "People are actually home giving tours of their house."

"I know. Next stop is the Armstrong place."

"I'm nervous about that," Trey admitted. "Especially with all these people around and what's up with Lyra? She seems sweet, but kind of uncomfortable."

"She used to be one of the popular girls, but none of us liked her much and now Brad is dating her. Or sleeping with her. I can't tell which one, but she's had a bit of a hard time lately. Her mom makes my mother look like a saint."

"I like Weezer," Trey said. "So where are we?"

"The Candlelight Inn. It's a new bed and breakfast. I'm not even sure it's open yet for business."

"It looks like a nice enough place," Trey said.

"Come with us." Caleb tossed his arm around Trey. "We'll give you the real tour of this town."

Trey glanced over his shoulder. "Should I be scared?"

"Not of Caleb or Brooklyn, but you should be worried about Brooklyn's alpacas."

"Oh. I've heard Lucy screaming before," Trey said.

"Hey. Lucy doesn't scream," Brooklyn said as she looped her arm through Caleb's. "She's just letting you know she's in the vicinity and to pay attention."

"Right," Malbec said. "Lucy is the only one of the alpacas that scares me and trust me when I say, she's a real moody girl."

"I'll make sure I tell her you said that." Brooklyn laughed as she headed toward the bed and breakfast.

Growing up, Riesling had always liked Brooklyn. She'd always been kind to Riesling and sometimes even willing to let her listen to her heartbeat.

Malbec and Eliza Jane strolled up the path arm in arm, crazy in love.

And pregnant.

No one knew but Riesling, and it was all she could do not to bust out and tell the world she was so happy for her brother and his future bride. The wedding was only two weeks away and Riesling couldn't wait. It was time that her family started having some positive things to celebrate.

Brad jumped out in front of her with a smile and pointed to his brace on his arm.

"I'm glad to see you're taking all my advice," Riesling said.

"I might have been a little cocky, but I'm no fool."

He glanced over his shoulder. "Trey seems like a nice guy. How are things going with him?"

She narrowed her eyes. "What have you heard?"

"Malbec said you're dating him."

"And are you dating Lyra?"

"It's complicated," Brad said with a stupid smile.

"What about your daughter? Why didn't you tell anyone?"

Brad ran his good hand across his face. "Same answer. But she's here now and I'm doing the best I can, temporarily." He let out a long breath. "We best catch up to the rest of the group."

Riesling followed Brad up to the house where Lacey greeted everyone with a warm smile. They followed Lacey inside where she gave her little speech about the house and then raced off to talk to a few other guests.

"Anyone know who the dude is hanging out in the background?" Brad asked.

"Yeah. He's the guy who thinks he owns Lacey's dog," Riesling said. "His name is Dean. He's ex-military. My dad says he a good guy, but I haven't met him yet."

"Nor have I," Malbec piped in. "But dang, it smells like cookies in here."

Trey came up behind her and wrapped his arms around her waist. He pressed his lips against her cheek. "Has anyone noticed the stockings hanging in front of the fireplace?"

"What about them?" Brooklyn asked with a scrunched face.

"They're horrible," Trey said.

"I have to agree. Whoever knitted them needs some serious lessons." Riesling should feel strange about the affection that Trey had been showing her in front everyone on the bus, but she didn't. She actually enjoyed it as if this was all normal and natural.

"Thanks a lot, Riesling," Brooklyn said. "I made them."

"Oh shit. I'm sorry." Riesling covered her mouth.

Everyone burst out laughing, including Caleb, who got an elbow to his rib.

It was the little things that mattered and while tonight could prove to be life-changing for Trey, this particular moment in time served to show Riesling that Candlewood Falls was her home and this group was her people.

She was exactly where she belonged, with the people who cared for her the most. Nothing else mattered.

Time would take care of everything else.

Trey

"Are you okay?"

Trey barely heard the words that had tumbled from Riesling's pretty lips. He was too busy staring at all the Christmas lights that lit up the Armstrong home.

And what a beautiful house it was.

Everyone else in the crowd had raced to the front door and was already engaged with the hosts, but not Trey and Riesling.

Nope.

He needed a little more time to collect his thoughts.

"I'm fine," he said. "It's just weird to be here knowing for sure he's my birth father." He reached inside his coat pocket and fingered the paperwork he'd pulled from the wooden casket.

All in all, there had been twenty-six illegal adoptions.

His had been the last one.

Trey had learned that his mother, Janet Sprouse, had been unmarried and younger than Jimmy Armstrong and according to the detailed notes that Doctor Allison kept, she had no desire to keep her child.

None whatsoever.

"And that he knew that day we were at the diner," Trey added.

"My father told you that he couldn't repeat—"

"I don't have any issue with your dad over what happened that day or why he couldn't and still can't tell me about the conversation." That was the honest truth because if it were Trey in Carter's shoes, he would have done the same thing, hands down. "All the handwritten notes in that coffin are confusing. If I'm to believe all that Doctor Allison wrote, then my biological father would have taken me in, but my birth mother wanted nothing to do with me."

Riesling wrapped one arm around his waist. "They were having an affair. He was married with two kids and she was young."

"If I'm to believe the notes, she didn't love him." Trey tried to push all the details from his brain, but it had become impossible and that annoyed him. He didn't want to be tainted by all that information. It rolled around in his mind, festering like a bad cold, giving him all sorts of ideas about his birth parents that he had no idea whether they were true or not. "Everything in that file tells me that Jimmy Armstrong would have risked it all to keep me, but she couldn't be bothered."

"Would you have wanted her as a mother if she didn't want you?" Riesling asked.

"That's not the point." Trey took her hand and put one foot in front of the other, heading toward the front door where Nadine Armstrong waved to the busload of visitors. Butterflies floated around his stomach like wild beasts. Even if he didn't have the chance to have a conversation tonight with his biological father, at least the seed would be planted.

All of this would take time. And it wasn't about becoming a family.

He had that.

His mother, up until the day she'd died, loved him desperately and had given him the world.

And to this day, his father was his hero. There was a small part of Trey that felt as though he'd betrayed his dad by searching for his birth parents. It had never been about finding what he'd missed, because he never felt as though he'd been without anything his entire life.

It had simply been about two simple things.

Finding out about where he came from biologically.

And honoring his late mother's wishes.

He hoped his dad could understand that and he prayed that Jimmy Armstrong and his wife would also get that this wasn't about uprooting their lives. He didn't want to make things difficult for them, nor did he expect anything from Jimmy.

Same went for his birth mother.

Then again, he could tell himself that all day long, but if it were completely true, he wouldn't be standing at Jimmy Armstrong's front door.

"Hello, Riesling. How are you?" Nadine asked as she opened the front door. "Your brother and his beautiful future bride are just beaming with love. Your mother must be bursting with pride over the upcoming wedding." Nadine stepped aside, letting Trey and Riesling into the massive foyer. "I'm thrilled Jimmy and I will be able to attend."

"My mom and dad will be so happy to hear that,"

Riesling said. "You've met Doctor Trey Jefferson, haven't you?"

"Briefly, once." Nadine pursed her lips as she stretched out her arm. "Welcome to my home."

"It's absolutely exquisite. I love the holiday decorations." Trey took Nadine's hand and kissed the back of it.

"Thank you." She quickly jerked it back as if she'd been burned. "If you will excuse me. I should see what the rest of your party is up to." She turned on her heel and stomped off down the hallway.

"I got the impression she didn't like me in her house much," Trey said under his breath as he glanced around, taking in the Victorian ambiance. "I hope no house we ever live in is on this tour."

Riesling paused in the center of the living room and stared at him with a blank expression.

He cleared his throat. That hadn't come out like he planned. It might be a little too soon to be talking living together, though it had been something that had crossed his mind. "Any idea where Jimmy might be?"

"He usually greets the guests with Nadine," Riesling said.

"He must have seen me coming."

"It's possible," Riesling said. "I suspect he's somewhere that's behind the ropes. Let's try his office first."

"Lead the way." Trey controlled his breathing by making sure his slow intake matched his exhale. He needed to keep a level head.

"You're hurting my hand," Riesling whispered.

"Oh. Sorry." He eased up on his grip, but he didn't let go. Through all of this, she'd grounded him, keeping him from going off the rails. If it weren't for Riesling, he would have approached this delicate conversation much differently.

He slowed their pace as he examined the family photos in the hallway. He could see the resemblance between him and Jimmy's other children, especially his son Junior.

It was uncanny.

Trey turned the corner and swallowed his breath.

Jimmy sat at his desk, staring down at what Trey thought was a piece of paper. Jimmy leaned back and sighed. "I was wondering when you might show up." He waved his hand. "Please. Come in and shut the door behind you."

Riesling palmed his cheek. "I'll be right outside."

He kissed her, needing to feel her positive energy.

She slipped out into the hallway.

The sound of the door clicking shut echoed in his ears.

He rubbed the back of his neck as he inched closer to the desk.

Jimmy folded his hands on the wood surface. Staring at his eyes was like looking at a portal into the future. It was impossible to ignore the similarities now.

"How did you find out I was your father?" Jimmy asked, jumping right into the thick of things.

Trey had to give the man kudos for being direct.

"It wasn't easy. I didn't have a lot to go on except for a letter my mom had left me from Doctor Allison to my dad, which lead me to Candlewood Falls. I didn't know for sure until Riesling and I found the documentation of all the illegal adoptions that Allison facilitated which matched me to you and Janet Sprouse."

"I'd like those records."

"I understand you don't want this to get out. I'm sure everyone else who has a file that we unearthed doesn't want this to make the evening news. Neither does my father and I don't want to hurt anyone. However, what Doctor Allison did was illegal."

"Perhaps that's true," Jimmy said. "When did you find those? Was it before or after my dinner with Carter River?"

"It was after. Why?" Trey stood in front of the desk as if he'd been a teenager and he'd been called to the principal's office.

"Will you kindly sit down?"

Trey glanced over his shoulder. There were two large leather chairs. He picked the one closer to the door. Gripping the armrests, he prepared himself to find the answers he wasn't so sure he wanted to know anymore.

"I had told Carter that night about you."

Trey's jaw slacked opened. He knew Carter had been keeping a great deal of information from him; however, he hadn't known the extent of it, and he certainly hadn't expected Jimmy to have confessed his bastard son.

"You've known I was your son this whole time?"

Jimmy pulled open a drawer and took out a thick folder and slid it across his desk. "I've known who you were your entire life. It was one of the things Allison did for some biological parents, if they paid extra."

"What are you talking about?" Trey took the file with a shaky hand. He sat on the edge of his seat and opened the folder, flattening it on the desk. He flipped through the pages, blinking wildly as his life played out in black and white.

"I wanted to know you had a good life. I needed to know Doctor Allison placed you with good people. And he did."

Trey pushed the papers toward Jimmy and leaned back. "What about Janet? Does she have something like this?"

"I doubt it. I didn't pay for her to have it because she didn't want it," Jimmy said. "And I haven't spoken to her since you were born."

That information hit Trey in the heart like a bullet and it wasn't just that Jimmy had no contact with Janet. It was the harsh tone in his voice that indicated pain and anger.

Not love.

"When I started this journey, I wanted to find out why my birth parents gave me up," Trey said.

Jimmy chuckled. "You'd think that's obvious in this case, but it's not."

"What do you mean?"

"I was willing to throw away my career and ruin my marriage to keep you. Janet was not."

"I did my research. She wasn't married, but she was a lot younger than you."

"That's true," Jimmy said. "And I shouldn't speak for her, but I doubt she'll meet with you, and if she does, she'll deny that she and I ever had an affair. Even if you put the proof in front of her, she'll lie and tell you she's not your birth mother."

"Why would she do that?" Trey asked.

"Mostly because of her current situation. She's happily married now with three kids. However, at the time of our affair, she didn't love me and she thought I ruined her life. She blamed me that she had to pause her education and leave Candlewood Falls."

"If she didn't love you, then why was she having an affair with you?"

"I bought her things," Jimmy said. "I didn't mind. I thought she and I had something special and believed someday we'd be together. I was a foolish man to ever believe that. Anyway, she hated being pregnant and when you were born, she wouldn't even look at you. I'm not saying this to be mean or to hurt you, but so that you will understand that sometimes when people go to extremes to bury secrets, there is a good reason." Jimmy swiped the tears that rolled down his cheek. "I got to hold you and I can remember every minute of my time with you. Personally, I've always wanted you in my life. I'm the anomaly in this situation. But I know others who used Doctor Allison, and that information you unearthed, it's going to hurt a lot of people."

"My intention isn't to hurt you, your family, my birth mother, or anyone else. I only wanted to know where I came from. I'm sitting here looking at you and it's obvious the biology is there. But I'm not your son. I'm Andrew Jefferson's boy. No one can change that."

"No. They can't." Jimmy nodded. "I'm sorry I ran out of that diner the other night. I knew we were going to have to have this conversation. But it wasn't going to be that night."

"May I ask you a question?"

"Of course."

"Does your wife know?" Trey asked.

"Yes," Jimmy said. "When I found out Janet was pregnant, I made the assumption, because my marriage wasn't all that great, that Janet and I were going to be together. I told Nadine and I had every intention of leaving her, but when Janet didn't want any of that, Nadine took me back, though it took a long time for us to find happiness. We fell madly in love with each other again. Things have been wonderful until—"

"I came to town," Trey said.

"It's not your fault. You're just the catalyst. The reminder of my affair." Jimmy tilted his head and smiled. "Only, I can't ever see you as a mistake. All I see is an amazing man that I helped create, but can't take credit for. The odd part is the first time I saw you strolling down Main Street, I felt an overwhelming sense of love. The same intense feeling I have for Junior, though it is different because I don't know you at all and I'd hope we can change that on any terms you choose."

"And what happens when the story of Doctor Allison's illegal adoption ring ends up on the news?"

"I'm not ashamed of you. I'm not worried about what this town will think of me. My wife will struggle a bit, but I know she'll get past it. She let you in this house and texted me you had arrived, so she's open to us having a relationship, if that's what you want," Jimmy said. "I am, however, concerned for those who have different life situations. Your birth mother being one of them."

A tap at the door startled Trey and he jumped.

"The bus is getting ready to leave for the next stop," Riesling said.

"I better go." Trey stood. "Thank you for seeing me and being honest."

"You're welcome."

Trey curled his fingers around the doorknob and twisted. He'd found his birth father. He knew who his birth mother was, and he'd uncovered an illegal adoption ring. "Maybe after the holidays we can have coffee."

"I'd like that," Jimmy said.

Trey stepped into the hallway and blew out a puff of air.

"Are you okay?" Riesling asked.

"I don't know." He took her into his arms and stared deep into her eyes. He cared for this woman more than he'd ever cared about anyone or anything. He understood Jimmy's willingness to give up everything for someone he loved. He'd do that for Riesling and her daughter. "We need to talk to your parents. Now."

17

RIESLING

iesling stared out the window as they pulled into her mother's home. "I want to see Ashling before we have this talk with my folks."

"I understand." Trey parked his vehicle and slipped from the driver's side. He'd been in a bit of a haze ever since they left the Victorian Christmas Tour.

"Hey." She raced to his side. "Just because your birth mother gave you up didn't mean she didn't care for you."

Trey narrowed his stare. "I'm not upset over that. I never have been. My parents loved me and I'm grateful for the life I've had. I wouldn't trade it for anything and if Janet doesn't want to know me, I'm okay with that."

"Then what's wrong?"

"It's the idea of using a child as a pawn to control someone. Nadine has done that with Jimmy his entire life. She made him choose between me and his other children. He even asked her to take me in and she said no."

"Can you blame her?"

"No. Actually, I can't. But she used her other children to get what she wanted."

"What do you mean?" Riesling asked.

"If Jimmy had any contact with me, she would leave him and poison his kids against him by telling them what he'd done." He reached out and tucked a few pieces of hair behind her ears. "I couldn't really understand what you were doing with Ashling and her father until now. You're a really good mother and I'm falling madly in love with you."

She opened her mouth, but no words came out. Only a gasp.

He smiled. "All that said. I still want Theo out of our lives."

"So do I," she managed to croak out. "I'm going through with the plan because he's hurt a lot of people and belongs in prison. I want to push him to sign over his parental rights."

"I'm worried about turning over what we found to the authorities and what will happen to your family and the winery."

"Let's go talk with my dad and find out what he thinks. Besides being a lawyer, he's pretty smart about all this stuff." She leaned in and kissed his cheek. "For the record, I'm falling in love with you too."

Carter

Carter lifted one of the letters and then dropped it like a hot potato. He was already fucking with evidence. He knew that.

He leaned back in his chair and closed his eyes. This winery meant the world to his wife and it was supposed to be the legacy they left their children. He'd even changed his last name so that his family could continue being the River family. Everything he and Weezer had revolved around family and the family business.

"Hey, sweetheart," Weezer said.

He blinked.

"Riesling and Trey are on their way over." She eased into one of the chairs across from the desk. "Riesling said Jimmy, for the most part, welcomed Trey."

"I'm not surprised." Sometimes knowing things that others didn't and not being able to repeat it sucked. Especially when he couldn't share that information with his wife. But she understood.

She always did.

"You're crinkling your forehead. Whenever you do that, it means you're struggling with a decision."

He nodded, waving his hand over the desk. "We do

the right thing and we could be implicated in an illegal adoption ring that we knew nothing about."

"What's the likelihood that will happen?"

"The implication is one hundred percent. Our address is the letterhead, and his office was on our property. Can it be proven that we knew anything? The last adoption happened thirty-five years ago when Andrew Jefferson and his wife adopted Trey. Could you and I have known? Sure. And we did hear stories of something being hidden, so there is that. The negative attention this will bring to our business could bankrupt us."

"And it will bring up Eliza Jane and her family."

Carter nodded. "Turning this over will bring down a shitshow on this family that we won't be able to control, not to mention the legalities that you and I could face. And then there are the people who went out of their way to make sure no one could find out they gave up a child, including that child. For example." Carter sorted through the papers until he found what he was looking for and handed it to his wife.

"Amanda Payne. Twenty-one years old. Gave birth to a baby boy." Weezer glanced over the paper. "Who is she?"

"A woman who worked for my father." Carter handed Weezer a second piece of paper. "As it turns out, she had an affair with my dad and they had a child."

"Good Lord," Weezer said.

"Unfortunately, that child passed away a few years

ago from cancer." Carter's throat choked up with emotion he hadn't been prepared to have for a half-sibling he had no idea even existed. It had been rumored his father had more than one affair and probably half a dozen bastard children across the country, but Carter always ignored the chatter.

"I'm sorry, honey."

"I have no idea what to do," Carter said. "If we sit on this and it ever comes to light, this family will never recover. But if we turn it over now, it could be just as bad. Regardless of what we do, you and I could wind up in jail."

A shadow appeared in the hallway. "Riesling and Trey must be here." Carter leaned forward.

"Not exactly," a male voice said with a hint of humor.

"Who's there?" Carter bolted out of his chair.

Theo appeared in the doorway with a smile and a weapon, pointed right at Weezer.

Carter's heart dropped to the pit of his stomach. He jumped around the desk and pushed himself in front of his wife. "What the fuck are you doing here?"

"To get some money and you're going to give it to me," Theo said.

"No. I'm not."

"Oh. I think you are." Theo raised his weapon. "To the tune of one million dollars. And you're going to give me all that evidence you were just talking about. That's going to be my insurance policy."

"We don't have that kind of money," Carter said.

"You're going to have to find it." Theo stepped into the office. "And soon, otherwise, you're going to regret it."

Carter let out a long breath. He had no way of getting word to Trey or Riesling to tell them to grab Ashling, who was upstairs watching a movie, and go to the police station.

"It's going to take some time."

"I'll take a seat and wait," Theo said. "But if you try anything funny, I'll go take my daughter and leave and you won't stop me."

Trey

Trey knew the second he walked into the house that shit wasn't right. But he hadn't expected to find Theo lurking around the hallways. Quickly, Trey tugged Riesling into one of the spare bedrooms on the first floor. "Hey," he whispered. "Go get Ashling and then go straight to Malbec's. From there, call the cops."

"What? Why? What's going on? You're scaring me," she said with wide eyes.

"Theo's in the office with your parents."

"What?" she screeched.

Trey covered her mouth to keep her from making any more noise. "Please. Just do what I say." He handed her his keys. "Tell the police that Theo is armed and dangerous."

"I'm not leaving you," she said softly.

"We need to get Ashling out of here." He lowered his chin and arched both brows. "The last thing she needs is to be in the middle of a showdown."

"Okay." Riesling nodded. "Please, be careful."

"You too." He brushed his lips over hers in a quick, but meaningful kiss. "He's going to be out of our lives soon."

He watched as Riesling scurried up the stairs. Pulling out his cell, he texted his father, quickly explaining the situation at hand and asking him for help.

It was a long shot, but it could work.

Dad: *I need about fifteen minutes to set it up. No problem.*

Trey: *That's it?*

Dad: *You had me start on this for real. Doing a ghost account won't be that hard. Trust me. I've got your back.*

Trey: *Thanks, Dad. I owe you one.*

He paused with his back to the wall so he could hear what was going on in the office. Out of the corner of his eye, he saw Riesling tugging her daughter toward the front door.

Thank God.

"The winery isn't that liquid," Carter said. "I don't have more than a couple hundred grand that I can get you tonight and even that is going to take me at least an hour."

"One million dollars," Theo said. "Or I take those documents and send them to the authorities and tell the world that you aided Doctor Allison for years with his illegal adoption scam. That you profited from it. And the courts will then give me full custody of my daughter."

"That's never going to happen," Trey said, stepping into the office.

Weezer gasped from her perch behind the desk.

Carter stood behind her with his hands on her shoulders and stared at Trey with wide eyes.

Theo turned his head, but kept the gun pointed at Weezer's chest. "Who the fuck—oh, the doctor. I've seen you around my ex. Are you fucking her?"

Carter growled.

"Not exactly the words I'd use." Trey leaned against the doorjamb and folded his arms as if he didn't have a care in the world. However, his heart beat so fast he thought he might have a heart attack. "And you're never getting custody of Ashling."

"Oh, yes, I am. Just like they are paying me a million dollars or going to jail."

"Weezer and Carter aren't going to jail either." Trey was having too much fun, and he shouldn't be, not when there was a loaded weapon in the room that was now pointed at his face. "But I'll be happy to give you the million dollars. I can even have it wired to you right now."

"Where would you get that kind of money?" Theo asked. "And why would you do that for these people?"

Trey wasn't about to answer either of those questions. He held up his phone. "Here's proof I have the money. All I need is your banking information."

Theo inched closer. "What's the catch?"

"Carter, could you get the parental rights papers?" Trey held his breath while Carter opened his top drawer and set a document on the wood surface, along with a pen. "Sign that and I'll give you the money right now."

"What is this?" Theo tilted his head as he glanced between the papers and Trey.

"A document stating that you give up all parental rights to Ashling. You're agreeing to never see or contact her again. Essentially, you're stating you don't want to be her father."

"What the fuck. Why would I do that?" Theo lifted the papers into his hand.

"Because you want that money," Trey said. "You need it to buy yourself out of trouble and I'll sweeten this deal for you. I'll make it two million." He tapped on his phone. "Now sign the papers and you can walk out of this house and we never have to see each other again."

"How do I know you won't fuck me over?" Theo

took the pen. His hand hovered over the legal documents.

"You can hit the *transfer funds* button. All I need you to do is put in the banking information and it's done."

Theo reached for the phone.

"Sign the papers," Trey said.

"I want the money first." Theo raised his weapon and thrust it toward Weezer.

"I'll put my cell on the table open to the transfer page. You sign. You take the money. I don't want to fuck you over. I just want you out of Riesling's life for good. And don't think about coming back because you won't have any leverage."

"Two million dollars is a good reason to stay away." Theo scribbled his signature on all the pages that Carter pointed to, then he picked up the phone, as well as his, and input his banking information. "Done." He held his phone over the desk and snapped a picture. "You try to take me down, this picture goes to the authorities."

"You can have your insurance policy." Trey held up his hand when Weezer opened her mouth. "It's time for you to leave. I'll be happy to escort you to the door."

"I know my way out." Theo smiled as he tucked his cell into his back pocket and practically skipped out of the office.

"Stay here. I'll be right back," Trey said.

"I'm not exactly sure what just happened," Weezer said. "And while I'm glad he signed that, I'm not sure I like the way this—"

"Trust me." Trey took off down the hallway, following Theo, who had taken his weapon and put it in his coat pocket.

Theo glanced over his shoulder. "I can't even begin to understand why you did this. I mean, she's not that great of a fuck."

"Maybe she's not the problem."

Theo paused midstep by the front door. "Are you looking to get your ass kicked?"

"Not really."

"Then I'd recommend keeping your fucking mouth closed." Theo pulled open the front door.

The sound of guns being engaged echoed in Trey's ears.

"Theo Richardson. Toss out your weapon and put your hands in the air," a male voice shouted. "The place is surrounded. There is no way out."

"What the fuck is this?" Theo held his hands to his sides. "Who told them I was here?"

"Not me," Trey said. "But if I were you, I'd do as they say. It looks like there's an entire SWAT team out there."

"This isn't going to stick," Theo mumbled as he pulled his weapon out, dropped it to the floor, and kicked it outside.

Three officers stormed the threshold.

One of them forcefully pushed Theo to the wall and patted him down before cuffing him and reading him his rights.

The entire scene was too good to be true.

Trey inched closer. "Oh. And by the way. I didn't wire any money. It was a dummy account. Besides, even if I had, that large of a transfer would have caused a huge red flag and it would have been held up for a good three days."

"You're going down for this. You and everyone in this family," Theo said under his breath.

Heavy footsteps rattled the floorboards.

"I doubt that," Carter said. "Can someone please get that piece of shit out of my wife's house."

"Yes, sir," one of the officers said. "We will need a statement from all of you."

"Can we do it in the morning?" Carter asked.

"Of course," the officer said.

"I'll make sure we come down first thing." Carter nodded and then closed the door.

"Where's my daughter?" Carter asked.

"I sent her and Ashling to Malbec and Eliza Jane's," Trey said. "We should probably call them and tell them that it's over."

Carter nodded. "You saved my family's life. I have no idea how to repay you."

Trey ran a hand across his scruffy face. "I can think of one thing."

"What's that?"

"Don't run me out of town when I tell you that I love your daughter."

18

NEW YEAR'S EVE...
RIESLING

Riesling leaned against the bar and waved to her little girl as she danced with Trey. Ashling had never looked so happy before.

She loved Trey and he adored her.

"He's a keeper," Malbec whispered in her ear.

She jumped.

"You freaking scared me."

Malbec laughed. "You haven't stopped daydreaming since Theo was arrested and Trey told you he loved you."

Her heart swelled. Life had taken so many wild twists and turns.

But there was still one big problem.

The illegal adoptions and the scandal that they were going to create. And since they turned over all the evidence to the authorities, she knew when the story came out, her family was going to suffer.

However, that hadn't been her decision. It had been her parents' and Trey's. They all agreed that if they tried to bury the secret again, it would only be unearthed someday in the future and the next time, it would cause even more harm because they had known.

"I'm not in fantasyland," she said. "I'm finally living in the real world." She hip checked her brother. "Now that you're married, when are you going to tell Mom and Dad that Eliza Jane is pregnant?"

He leaned over Riesling's shoulder and pointed. "We just did."

"Oh, jeez. Poor Eliza Jane. Mom is going to drive her batshit crazy."

"The good news is that Mom is going to push her to slow down and I'm going to agree, which will give Chablis some room to come into the fold."

"I don't know why Chablis is feeling so alienated. You want her help and so does Mom."

"It's because she was never given the chance to do things by herself and I can understand that. It was always me at the helm with all of us playing a role, or none of us, and Chablis took that as she wasn't good enough."

"That's bullshit, but it all might be for nothing when this adoption scandal—"

"We've got nothing to worry about." Her father waltzed over with a bottle of wine in his hand. "I wasn't going to say anything until tomorrow, but with babies and other happy news, I might as well let the cat out of the bag."

"What's going on with the illegal adoption case?" Malbec asked.

"Wait. I want Trey to hear this." Riesling waved to the love of her life.

He nodded and took Ashling by the hand.

"What's going on?" Trey asked.

"Ashling, baby girl," her father said. "Did you hear you're going to be a big cousin?"

"What? No. Who's having a baby?"

"Auntie Eliza Jane and I are." Malbec ruffled her head. "Why don't you go over there and congratulate her."

"Okay." Ashling took off running.

"I guess this is a serious conversation." Trey climbed up on a bar stool and pulled Riesling between his legs. He wrapped his arms around her body and kissed her temple.

"It is, but it's all good," her father said. "I heard from the district attorney this morning."

"Oh?" Riesling's heart pounded. "And?"

"Since Allison is dead, they can't prosecute him and he acted alone, or at least they believe he did. After interviewing people like Trey's father, they won't be bringing charges against those who used the services. As far as reuniting children with their birth parents, that will be done only if all parties want it and on a case-by-case basis," her father said.

"That's good news." Trey squeezed her shoulder. "But that doesn't mean your family won't be dragged through the mud. It's going to be hard to keep this kind of thing out of the news. My father is doing his best, but it's a big story."

"We know that and that's why Weezer and I want him to break the story on our terms. Well, on yours too. If you're willing to tell it."

Riesling turned and stared into Trey's eyes. "Would you want to do that?"

"I'd need to talk to my dad. And Jimmy. But I'd be open to it if you all think it's what's best for our family."

Riesling smiled. It had been a long time since she'd felt part of her own family and now she had Trey as well.

Things were still new. But they were going well.

The practice was booming and their relationship was developing into something she'd only thought happened in fairy tales.

"You should do it right now," Malbec said. "You're not taking anything away from mine and Eliza Jane's day. Trust me."

"I agree," Carter said. "Did you bring it with you?"

"I've been carrying it with me wherever I go for three days," Trey said. "Are you sure?"

"Oh, hell yes." Malbec slapped Trey on the back before jogging across the dance floor to where the band had set up.

"What are you all babbling about?" Riesling asked.

"You're about to find out," her father said.

"Ladies and gentlemen," Malbec's voice came over the sound system. "If you could all please direct your attention over there to my sister Riesling. Thank you."

"What the hell is going on?" Riesling glared at Trey as he stepped around her and dug his hand into his pocket. Butterflies filled her stomach. She flattened her hand over her midriff. "Trey? What are you doing?"

"Hang on a second," he said. "Ashling. Where are you?"

"Right here!" Ashling skipped across the dance floor, skidding to a stop about two feet away.

He lowered himself to her level and placed a small box in her hands. "I'm going to ask your mom a question. But it's also for you because I love you just as much."

"I love you too," Ashling said with a beaming smile.

"Oh shit," Riesling mumbled as she tried to catch her breath. Her pulse raced wildly out of control. He wasn't going to do this here. Now. With everyone watching.

He raised his hand. Between his thumb and forefinger was a shiny diamond ring.

Yup. He was.

"I never expected to fall in love when I came to Candlewood Falls, but I did. And I couldn't be happier. I want to spend the rest of my life, right here, with you and Ashling. What do you say? Will you marry a small-town doctor?"

"Mommy, say yes." Ashling jumped up and down. "Can I open my gift?"

"As soon as Mommy answers you can," Trey whispered.

"Yes. A million times, yes." Riesling tossed her arms around him and kissed him. Hard.

The sound of hands clapping filled the night air.

"Mommy. Mommy!" Ashling tugged at her dress. "Look at this."

Riesling lifted her little girl and stared at the pendant necklace dangling in her pudgy little fingers. "What's inside?"

"It's a picture of all three of us. Like a real family." Ashling sniffled.

"We are a real family," Riesling said.

"I'd like to make that even more official," Trey said. "I know it will be a while before we can do this. But your father has the paperwork. I want to *legally* adopt Ashling."

Riesling swallowed a guttural sob. Coming home had been the best decision she'd ever made.

"I love you, Trey. Ever since you walked into my life, it's been nothing short of spectacular."

EPILOGUE
VALENTINE'S DAY...

Trey

T rey stood by the river's edge in his suit. There had been a fresh snowfall the night before; however, the sun had come out and the temperatures had risen to close to fifty, creating a beautiful backdrop for a wedding.

"I've never seen you so nervous," Malbec, his best man, said.

"Well, let's see here. I'm getting married, for starters. Your mother has taken over the wedding, not allowing either Riesling or me to have any say, and both my father and my birth father are here for the first time. I think you'd be a ball of nerves too."

Malbec laughed. "It could be worse."

"I don't see how."

Before Malbec could come back with any kind of retort, the cello player began.

Trey blew out a puff of air and turned. He grabbed Malbec's arm. "That's Riesling?"

"You don't recognize your future wife?" Malbec laughed way too loud.

Riesling held her father's arm and she walked down the makeshift aisle wearing her mother's wedding dress. It was a simple white dress with a fur shawl and this white mesh thing for a headpiece.

She wore the pearl necklace that he'd given her last week as an early wedding present. She was the most beautiful creature he'd ever laid eyes on. Her kind heart and sweet soul sucked him in, and he was hers forever.

Carter shook his hand. "You take good care of my girl."

"Yes, sir," Trey said with thick emotion as he took Riesling's hand. "You look gorgeous."

"You don't look so bad yourself," she said.

"I'm going to love you forever," he whispered.

"You better." She smiled.

Trey stared into her eyes and barely heard the justice of the peace as he went through the motions of the ceremony. They had opted for family only and a quick wedding. Not because they were worried about the cold; they didn't care about that. But because they were more interested in the being married and spending the rest of their lives together part.

"You may kiss your bride," the justice of the peace said.

Trey felt as though he were kissing her for the first time. It was slow, tender, and sweet, and he never wanted it to end. But a little girl was tugging at her mother's dress.

"Did you tell him, Mommy?" Ashling asked.

"Tell me what?"

"I'm going to be a big sister!" Ashling jumped up and down and ran in a circle around them, giggling.

"Ashling," Carter called. "Come here."

"I think she's confusing cousin with sister," Trey said.

Riesling took his hand and pressed it over her middle. "No, honey. She's not. She knew exactly what she was talking about."

"Excuse me?"

"You're going to be a daddy."

Goosebumps dotted his skin. He opened his mouth, but he couldn't form any words. He tried to clear his throat; however, it was too dry.

"Trey. Are you okay?" Riesling palmed his cheek.

"I'm better than okay." He lifted her off the ground and twirled her around. "I'm the luckiest man in the world. I have the perfect wife, a beautiful daughter, and now we're going to have another baby. I don't know what I did to deserve you." He set her feet on the snowy ground and kissed her like they were the only two people standing on the river's edge.

This was where he belonged.
This was home.

Thank you for taking the time to read *The Buried Secret*. Please feel free to leave an honest review. Next in the series is: *Its In His Kiss*. And please check out the rest of the series:

Lips Of An Angel
Kisses Sweeter than Wine
A Little Bit Whiskey

Grab a glass of vino, kick back, relax, and let the romance roll in…
Sign up for my Newsletter *(https://dl.bookfunnel.com/ 82gm8b9k4y) where I often give away free books before publication.*

Join my private Facebook group (https://www.facebook.com/ groups/191706547909047/) where I post exclusive excerpts and discuss all things murder and love!

READY FOR ANOTHER TRIP TO CANDLEWOOD FALLS?

For more Alpachino the Alpaca antics and to find out who went to prison for killing Sam's Father's read <u>TAKING ROOT</u> by Stacey Wilk.

And the second book in Stacey's series...What will Brad Wilde the man who has it all do when an orphan is dropped on his doorstep? RAISING WINTER by Stacey Wilk.

Also by Stacey Wilk in this series: Even the most unexpected circumstances may teach us how to forgive what cannot be changed. DEFINING CHANCES.

And While packing away her mothers life, Petra Wilde discovers a life of her own in BEGINNING OVER.

If you want to spend some time with Sam Wilde and his quest for an apple to make you happy and horny you'll want to read WILDE TEMPTATION by K.M. FAWCETT.

And the second book in K.M. Fawcett's series...Spend the holidays with Lacey Wilde, her dog Remi, and a sexy marine who claims Remi belongs to him in <u>WILDE CHRISTMAS</u> by K.M. Fawcett.

Also by K.M. Fawcett is WILD IN LOVE: Can a bad boy and a good girl overcome their fears to find true love?

And in WILDE TREASURES: While searching for a hidden fortune, can two lonely adventurers discover some treasurers are more precious than gold.

ACKNOWLEDGMENTS

A big thank you to Stacey Wilk and K.M. Fawcett for inviting me into Candlewood Falls.

———

ABOUT THE AUTHOR

Jen Talty is the *USA Today* Bestselling Author of Contemporary Romance, Romantic Suspense, and Paranormal Romance. In the fall of 2020, her short story was selected and featured in a 1001 Dark Nights Anthology.

Regardless of the genre, her goal is to take you on a ride that will leave you floating under the sun with warmth in your heart. She writes stories about broken heroes and heroines who aren't necessarily looking for romance, but in the end, they find the kind of love books are written about :).

She first started writing while carting her kids to one hockey rink after the other, averaging 170 games per year between 3 kids in 2 countries and 5 states. Her first book, IN TWO WEEKS was originally published in 2007. In 2010 she helped form a publishing company (Cool Gus Publishing) with *NY Times* Bestselling Author Bob Mayer where she ran the technical side of the business through 2016.

Jen is currently enjoying the next phase of her life...the empty nester! She and her husband reside in Jupiter, Florida.

Grab a glass of vino, kick back, relax, and let the romance roll in...

Sign up for my _Newsletter (https://dl.bookfunnel.com/82gm8b9k4y)_ where I often give away free books before publication.

Join my private _Facebook group_ (https://www.facebook.com/groups/191706547909047/) where I post exclusive excerpts and discuss all things murder and love!

Never miss a new release. Follow me on Amazon:amazon.com/author/jentalty

And on Bookbub: bookbub.com/authors/jen-talty

ALSO BY JEN TALTY

Everyone needs a SAFE HARBOR!

Mine To Keep

Mine To Save

Mine To Protect

Mine to Hold

Mine to Love

Check out LOVE IN THE ADIRONDACKS!

Shattered Dreams

An Inconvenient Flame

The Wedding Driver

Clear Blue Sky

Blue Moon

Before the Storm

NY STATE TROOPER SERIES (also set in the Adirondacks!)

In Two Weeks

Dark Water

Deadly Secrets

Murder in Paradise Bay

To Protect His own

Talon's Honor

Arthur's Honor

Rex's Honor

Kent's Honor

Buddy's Honor

Aegis Network Short Stories

Max & Milian

A Christmas Miracle

Spinning Wheels

Holiday's Vacation

The Brotherhood Protectors

Out of the Wild

Rough Justice

Rough Around The Edges

Rough Ride

Rough Edge

Rough Beauty

The Brotherhood Protectors

The Saving Series

Saving Love

Saving Magnolia

Saving Leather

Hot Hunks

Cove's Blind Date Blows Up

My Everyday Hero – Ledger

Tempting Tavor

Malachi's Mystic Assignment

Needing Neor

Holiday Romances

A Christmas Getaway

Alaskan Christmas

Whispers

Christmas In The Sand

Heroes & Heroines on the Field

Taking A Risk

Tee Time

A New Dawn

The Blind Date

Spring Fling

Summers Gone

Winter Wedding

The Awakening

Fated Moons

The Collective Order